THE INCREDIBLY DEAD PETS OF REX DEXTER

NARWHAL I'M AROUND

THE INCREDIBLY
DEAD

PETS

OF REX DEXTER

NARWHAL I'M AROUND

AARON REYNOLDS

(L B)

LITTLE, BROWN AND COMPANY

New York Boston

Copyright © 2021 by Aaron Reynolds

Cover art copyright © 2021 by Hugo Cuellar. Cover design by Jenny Kimura. Cover copyright © 2021 by Hachette Book Group, Inc.

Little, Brown and Company
Hachette Book Group
1290 Avenue of the Americas, New York, NY 10104
Visit us at LBYR.com

First Edition: May 2021

Little, Brown and Company is a division of Hachette Book Group, Inc. The Little, Brown name and logo are trademarks of Hachette Book Group, Inc.

The publisher is not responsible for websites (or their content) that are not owned by the publisher.

Library of Congress Cataloging-in-Publication Data
Names: Reynolds, Aaron, 1970- author.
Title: Narwhal I'm around / Aaron Reynolds.
Other titles: Narwhal I am around
Description: First edition. | New York ; Boston: Little, Brown and Company, 2021. | Series: The incredibly dead pets of Rex Dexter; 2 | Audience: Ages 8-12. | Summary: "Sixth grader Rex Dexter uses his ability to communicate with dead animals to investigate a narwhal's mysterious death"—Provided by publisher.
Identifiers: LCCN 2020053587 | ISBN 9780759555235 (hardcover) | ISBN 9780759554535 (ebook) | ISBN 9780759554528 (ebook other)
Subjects: CYAC: Ghosts—Fiction. | Marine animals—Fiction. | Friendship—Fiction. | Mystery and detective stories.
Classification: LCC PZ7.R33213 Nar 2021 | DDC [Fic]—dc23
LC record available at https://lccn.loc.gov/2020053587

ISBNs: 978-0-7595-5523-5 (hardcover), 978-0-7595-5453-5 (ebook)

Printed in the United States of America

LSC-C

Printing 1, 2021

To Daxter

PROLOGUE

Let's get a few things out of the way.

My name is Rex Dexter.

And I am cursed.

I am cursed with brains, ingenuity, a can-do attitude, and more than my fair share of devilish good looks.

But also with an actual curse.

Prepare yourself. What follows is not for the faint of heart:

I can see and talk to dead animals.

There. Now you know.

How did this happen? Some might blame the Grim Reaper in a malfunctioning carnival game. Some might blame my parents for giving me a chicken for my birthday. Some might blame my own tendency to leap before I look.

I blame my best friend, Darvish.

Regardless of where the blame lies (Darvish), this has led to a plethora of recently deceased animals appearing to me, tethered to this mortal coil until their unfinished business has been resolved. I have done my level best to aid these dead and earthbound members of the animal kingdom who keep showing up to my bedroom uninvited.

Lucky for them, my pluck and derring-do have more than proven worthy to the task. With the help of my faithful (dead) chicken and an unreliable (alive) Darvish, I recently helped an entire gaggle of endangered zoo animals capture their assassin. You've heard of the recent Middling Falls Zoo Murders?

No? Pity. It is a riveting tale.

Rest assured, the culprit has been apprehended and now awaits his day in court. Thanks to me. For more details, see Book One of my published works.

Having recently vanquished this criminal mastermind, I took the night off to recharge my batteries. I attended the Evening of Enchantment Dance at my school.

This has turned out to be a huge mistake. What started out as an evening of well-earned frivolity has led to a troubling and unforeseen predicament:

I think I might accidentally have a girlfriend.

I do not want to talk about it.

1

I have just returned from the school dance and lived to tell the tale. Perhaps at some point, I will regale you with the lurid details. For now, the horror is still too fresh.

Suffice it to say, my feet hurt. I am emotionally frazzled. And I want to go to bed.

The last thing I want to do right now is argue with a dead chicken.

So imagine my dismay when I reach my bedroom and find myself arguing with one.

"Welcome home, buddy!" cries Drumstick, flapping his wings. "Where have you been?"

"Move, Drumstick," I tell him. "I want to put my head under my pillow."

Over the past few weeks, this dead chicken has proven himself a loyal and helpful sidekick. Possibly even a friend.

But right now, he is obstructing my bedroom door.

He's dripping green ghost-mist all over the hallway carpet.

And he's standing between me and my pillow. Which makes me want to turn him into a ghostly Happy Meal, despite his helpful nature.

"I don't think you want to go in there," he says.

"I do. Trust me."

"If you say so," says the chicken. "But you've got a visitor. He's been waiting in your beanbag chair all night."

This stops me cold. I can feel the ghost-chill of the

freshly dead seeping through the crack under the door. Some spirit lurks within.

"He's in there," says the chicken ominously. "He's really grumpy. And he's got a weapon."

I turn to Drumstick. "What is it?"

"The weapon?" asks Drumstick. "Or the animal?"

"The animal," I clarify.

"I dunno." Helpful. "I tried to keep him busy while you were gone. We played Monopoly! He doesn't understand what money is, so that didn't last long."

"Well, did you question him?" I ask. "Did you conduct a thorough interrogation in my absence?"

"Oh yeah! You betcha!" says Drumstick, nodding eagerly.

That's a relief. I wasn't 100 percent sure my sidekick had it in him. "What did you learn?"

He scratches his beak with his flipper-like wing. "He's some kind of fish, I think."

I sigh. If you learn nothing else from my escapades, take heed of this: Don't leave a dead chicken in charge of your bedroom while you go to the Evening of Enchantment Dance. Also, don't go to the Evening of Enchantment Dance.

Words to live by.

I grab the doorknob. I wipe my face with my tie. And I open the door.

2

My room smells like a tuna sandwich.

This should come as no surprise. Because what greets me is a two-thousand-pound narwhal.

They are not at all cute like deceitful plushie vendors and children's book illustrators would have you believe. Do not be taken in. This thing is freaky weird. And just sitting in my beanbag chair like he owns the place.

"Well, at least you dressed professionally," he mutters as I walk in. "It's the least you could do after you kept me waiting all night."

A seven-foot horn sprouts from his head, jutting toward my ceiling fan like some medieval lance.

There was a time when I would have been shocked

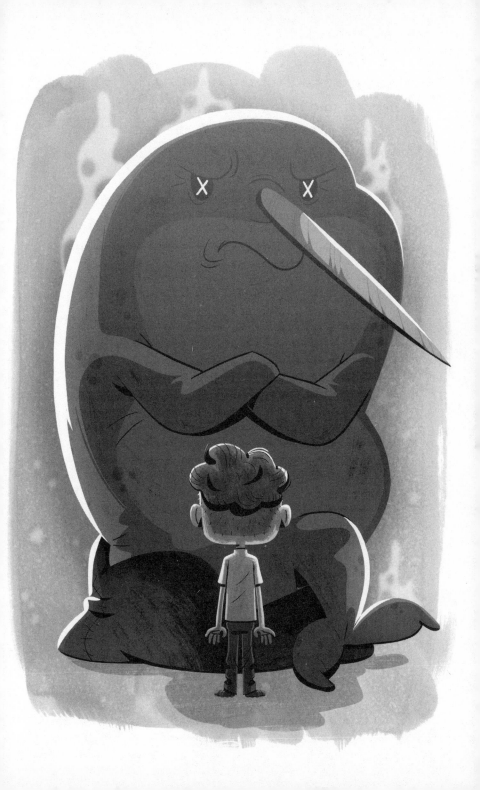

at the appearance of such an unsettling phantom lounging in my furniture. Ah, the days of my youth.

"Hi," I say, trying to smooth the tension with my disarming charm. "Sorry about the wait. I had a prior engagement."

"Well, I've been dead all night!" he grouses. "I show up to see the one guy who can do something about it, and that goofy seagull tells me that he's not available. And beats the pants off me at a board game! Talk about adding insult to injury!"

"You don't have pants," I point out. If you've ever tried to reason with a fish, you know it's a futile undertaking. But I try anyway. "To be fair, now that you're dead, don't you pretty much have nothing but time on your hands?"

"I don't have hands!" he huffs back.

Fair point. He crosses his fins over his chest and pouts. He's grayish white, except for the spooky green mist that seems to accompany every one of these beasties that return from the dead. He lashes his tail dramatically.

"Well, I'm here now," I say.

"Then help me!" he cries. Now that he's dropped the tough-guy routine, he just looks like a really scared fish. "I don't know what's going on!"

"You died," I prompt him.

"Yeah!" he cries.

"And now you can't move on?" I ask.

"That's right!" he exclaims. "It's like I'm spiritually..."

"Tethered?" I suggest.

"I was going to say constipated," says the narwhal. "But yeah. Tethered, too. Constipated and tethered. And once I knew I was dead and I knew I was stuck, I somehow just knew to come here."

"Lucky me," I say.

"Did you get run over by a big steamroller?" asks Drumstick.

"No," he says.

"Ugh." Drumstick shakes his head. "That's how I went. Not fun."

"What's a steamroller?" he asks.

"Big squashy thing," says the chicken.

"Not relevant," I say, nudging Drumstick.

"Not relevant!" the chicken tells the narwhal.

"How did it happen?" I ask.

"I can't remember much," he says. "But I remember one thing. Right at the very end."

"And what's that?" I prompt.

A shiver runs through him. "Bad water."

3

Was this narwhal poisoned? Was he a victim of pollution or some environmental catastrophe? Did somebody slip something into his Kool-Aid when he wasn't looking?

The narwhal offers no further explanation. He says it's too soon. He needs emotional space.

So I am left with nothing to go on but *bad water*. It's a cryptic message. Some would call it impossible to decipher.

And on this night, it robs me of my sleep. That, and the narwhal snores.

This fish and his bad-water problems are not the only things wreaking havoc on my much-needed rest. The roadblocks are numerous.

Roadblock One: this accidental-girlfriend situation. It preys on my mind night and day. I'll say no more. Quit asking.

Roadblock Two: The weekend is half over. Which means Monday looms. Which means school. Which means I will have to deal, once again, with Ms. Yardley.

I have a love-hate relationship with my teacher. She loves to boss me around. And I hate that. I am forced to spend the best hours of my precious youth under her alleged tutelage. There should be a law.

Roadblock Three: Drumstick eats in bed and keeps leaving crumbs in my bedsheets. It is troubling. And itchy.

With this many distractions preying on my mind, it is no wonder I cannot rest nor make heads or tails of this narwhal's perplexing situation.

But I should not worry.

I have successfully freed five other dead animals from the shackles that bind them to this world. And I will triumph again.

The formula for my success is simple.

Every great mind needs a sounding board. Some poor sap they can talk at. A compatriot they can unload on. A boon companion they can spew ideas upon, until the continuous stream of word vomit leads to a brilliant solution.

It's called auditory processing.

Sherlock Holmes had Watson. Batman had Alfred. Ronald McDonald had Grimace. Or the Hamburgler. Or that weirdo with a cheeseburger for a head.

I have Darvish. Only, Darvish seems to be dodging my calls this weekend. So I find myself once again held at bay from my own genius.

As you can see, the cosmos conspire against me. It's a shame. Because it's the animals who suffer.

Darvish had better watch it. He is coming dangerously close to being named Roadblock Four. At which point, I may have to replace him as my sounding board.

I wonder if that cheeseburger-head guy is available.

4

I forgot to mention Roadblock Five: my loving parents. Who have taken me out to Sunday dinner.

"Why are we at this weird restaurant?" I ask.

There are several forks in front of me. Candlelight flickers from the center of the table, obviously a ploy to save this dive from paying for costly electricity. Also, dim lighting makes it easy to get away with unsanitary conditions. I carefully avoid the chilled water in the crystal goblet before me. After all, bad water is killing narwhals. You can't be too careful.

"It's not a weird restaurant," my dad says defensively.

"It's a fancy restaurant," says my mom. "We're celebrating!"

"Celebrating what?" I say. "My birthday was just last month."

"Your mom got a new job!" my dad says.

I turn to her with interest. "Are you finally becoming a pastry chef? Because anything else is a step down if you ask me."

"No, I'm not becoming a pastry chef," she says.

Honestly. What do I have to do to get more key lime pie in my life?

"I'm the financial advisor to Trinity Bellingham."

The tuxedo-wearing waiter brings the food and gently sets the plates in front of us. But I am too distracted to notice.

"Trinity Bellingham?" I ask. "Hold on. You're working for Dimitri Bellingham's mom?"

"That's right," says my mom.

"Wait, who's Dimitri Bellingham?" my dad asks.

"Who's Dimitri Bellingham? Only the richest kid in Middling Falls," I inform him.

"Well, excuse me," says my dad. "Is he a buddy of yours?"

"He is in the grade below me," I explain. "And he is buddies with nobody. The children of Middling Falls School give him a wide berth. And with good reason. He is weird."

"Weird how?" asks my mom.

"He arrives to school in a limousine. He has two bodyguards that surround him at lunchtime. Everybody is scared to get too close. Those goons look like they could stomp your average sixth grader into bean paste."

"Aw," says my mom sympathetically. "That must be really lonely for him."

"His mom is a billionaire. He has his money to keep him company." I sniff my plate cautiously. "Wait, you're working for her?"

"That's right," she says with a grin.

"Excellent," I cry, rubbing my hands together. "So, can I expect my allowance to increase commensurate with your newfound success?"

"You don't get an allowance, Rex," my dad points out.

"True," I agree. "An injustice that has gone on far too long. Five hundred dollars a week sounds like an ideal starting rate."

My mother laughs. I fail to see the humor in the

situation. "My boss is a billionaire. That doesn't mean we are now."

"It's a big deal for your mom," Dad says.

"Well, congratulations, then," I say, toasting her with my goblet but being careful not to drink. "However, if I'm reading the situation correctly, I am still without money or a steady supply of pie. I have demands on my time, people. I face complex issues you cannot begin to fathom. I can't afford to be pulled away willy-nilly to dine upon dimly lit cuisine."

My dad sighs and shakes his head. "Just eat your lobster mac and cheese."

"It looks yummy, Rex," my mom says, looking at my plate.

"I'm sure it is," I tell her. "Except this fancy-pants restaurant has one big problem. I mean, besides defaulting on their electric bill."

My dad darts his eyes at me. "What's the problem, Rex?"

"It's the lobster mac and cheese." I push my plate away. "It has lobster in it."

Who ruins mac and cheese with seafood? Honestly.

5

Ms. Yardley is wily indeed.

Because when I enter my classroom on Monday, she has planted a decoy at her desk. It's a clever ruse to prevent me from talking to Darvish about the pressing matters at hand. A ploy to catch us all in some sort of tomfoolery. But it won't work.

I confront the imposter head-on. "You're in Ms. Yardley's seat."

She shoots me a lopsided grin. "I can see how you might think that," she says mysteriously. "For now, just take a seat." She wiggles her fingers in front of me like a magician performing a trick. "All will be revealed."

But I am not thrown off by her mysterious nature or

quirky lopsided smile. She is in cahoots with Ms. Yardley. As far as I'm concerned, she spells trouble.

When the bell rings, the woman stands. This lady is ripped. Muscular. Like, she could probably arm-wrestle the Hulk and at least tie. But before she can explain her presence or unexpected brawn, she is peppered with inquiries.

"Who are you?" asks Holly Creskin.

"What's going on?" asks Edwin Willoughby.

"Where's Ms. Yardley?" asks Sami Mulpepper.

"Hi, everybody," she says. "Don't worry. I will answer all your questions. I know it must be strange to find a new person sitting at your teacher's desk."

The woman gives the unruly mob another of her disarming smiles, and their questions grind to a halt.

My classmates. They are easily quelled.

There's Holly Creskin. She has a high-pitched voice, loves unicorns, and giggles far more than she should.

There's Edwin Willoughby. He is a flimflam man who skates by on good looks and cheap cologne.

There's Sami Mulpepper. I don't want to talk about her. I especially don't want to talk about her hair that is the color of dewdrops on marigolds. My reasons are my own.

They are all sheep. And they are easily fleeced by this woman who sits before us.

"My name is Miss Mary," she tells us. "I'm your new teacher."

"What happened to Ms. Yardley?" asks Darvish.

Miss Mary bites her lip. "As I understand, she's taking a little break."

This explanation may placate the masses, but I see through these code words. Ms. Yardley has finally snapped. Blown a gasket. Gone kooky. I knew it was only a matter of time.

"Does anyone have any other questions?" asks Miss Mary. "Anything is okay."

Daniel Grimmer raises his hand. "Why do you have so many muscles?"

Miss Mary shoots him an approving smile. "You noticed, huh? I'm an amateur wrestler."

"What does that mean?" Darvish asks.

"It means I could probably pick up my desk and throw it across the room," she says.

"Whoa!" The class titters in wonderment.

But I refuse to be intimidated. "What are those?" I ask, pointing behind her.

"Those are some of my championship wrestling belts," she tells us, waving at the enormous shiny buckles lining the credenza. "I'm very proud of them. Do any of you have anything you do for fun that you're proud of?"

The room fills with banal discussion about Little League teams and video game scores. I just turn to Darvish and shake my head in disgust.

"Can you believe this ruse?" I ask him.

"She seems nice," says Darvish. "And look. She has a cool tattoo on her arm."

"Don't be a stooge, Darvish," I tell him. "That's probably prison ink. Look, I could tell these people sordid tales of murdered animals that would put them off their Taco Tuesdays for a month. I could spin true-life ghost stories that would make their toes curl. I could put their petty accomplishments to shame with first-hand accounts of my recent supernatural exploits."

"Probably better not," says Darvish.

He's right, of course. Because that's how you wind up in the cuckoo house. With Ms. Yardley.

I raise my hand. "So, you'd like us to believe that your last name is Mary?"

She smiles. "That's right."

"That's a first name," I point out.

"Sometimes," she says good-naturedly.

"What's your first name?" I ask accusingly.

"Mary-Kate," she says.

"Your name is Mary-Kate Mary?"

"It is."

I shake my head. It's obvious this woman is hiding a dark past behind ill-conceived fabrications.

"That's a cool name," says Holly Creskin. "Jazzy."

The whole class nods in agreement.

Lemmings. I'm surrounded by lemmings.

6

Everybody needs a place where they can be themselves. Where they can bare their soul. Where they can let their hair down.

The lunchroom is not that place. It is a sad room with sticky seats. It is filled with the smell of maple syrup and despair. But it will have to do. Between the clatter of lunch-lady serving spoons and the general mayhem of pent-up schoolchildren, serious covert discussions can happen in plain sight. And nobody will be the wiser.

Unless Darvish shouts your personal business all over the cafeteria.

"What do you mean, you might accidentally have a girlfriend?!" cries Darvish, shouting my personal business all over the cafeteria. For reasons that should be obvious, I may now occasionally refer to him as Road-block Four. RB4 for short.

I turn to my best friend. "Would you pipe down and eat your noodles?"

"It's not noodles," he says, shoving a forkful into his mouth. "It's rice pulao."

This guy. As usual, he's focusing on the wrong thing.

"Besides," he says. "How can you accidentally have a girlfriend?"

I give him a glare that reinforces his ineptitude. "I am extremely charismatic. That's how."

"I mean the accidentally part," Darvish clarifies.

"The answer to that is easy, Darvish," I tell him. "I don't know. But this much I do know. I blame you."

"Me?"

"If you had been at the Evening of Enchantment Dance, this never would have happened."

"What *did* happen?" he asks between bites.

"I don't want to talk about it," I tell him.

"Well, you should have come with me instead of going to the dance," Darvish says, shaking his head. "I had fun at Iggy Graminski's house. He taught me this cool role-playing game called Monsters & Mayhem. We played all weekend!"

"Is that why I was unable to reach you?" I knock my head against the table in frustration. "Urgent matters are at hand and you're playing silly games?"

"Monsters & Mayhem isn't silly," he stresses. "It was awesome! Iggy is the GM, right? That stands for Game Master. And he led us through this dungeon where we had to fight off a massive band of bugbears..."

I grab his face in my hands to focus his wandering attention.

"Well, you're going to have to put all that on hold," I tell him. "We have a supernatural conundrum on our hands."

"What are you talking about?" And then realization dawns on the dim valley of his mind. "Wait!" he cries. "Another dead animal?!"

Darvish is the only person alive who knows about my special set of skills. I'd like to keep it that way. Which is hard with RB4 shooting his mouth off at full volume.

I scan the room nervously. But my classmates gab vapidly at nearby tables. Second graders across the cafeteria roughhouse and fling French Toast Stix at each other, blissfully unaware of the paranormal secrets being discussed right under their snotty little noses.

"Not here, Darvish," I tell him. "The walls have ears."

He looks around. "Well, these aren't really walls," he points out. "They're more like movable partitions."

"It doesn't matter," I tell him. "We'll talk about it after school."

"I've got homework to do," he says. "So do you."

Miss Mary may have everyone else fooled with her fancy wrestling belts and her laissez-faire attitude, but she doles out oodles of math homework just like every other teacher. Just another minion of the system.

"Don't worry," I tell Darvish. "I'll come to you. I'll bring the narwhal."

"Narwhal?!" he cries at the top of his lungs.

Poor kid. He doesn't understand the first thing about covert operations.

And then I spot something that sends a chill up my spine.

It's my girlfriend.

"I've gotta go." I do not want a scene. I stand, obscuring my face from view with a notebook. The key to escaping detection is to avoid eye contact. "You never saw me."

Trouble is, this strategy also makes it very easy to trip and fall headfirst into a large plastic tub.

A tub filled to the brim with French Toast Stix.

And despair.

7

Darvish's parents adore me.

Which is good. Because my dead narwhal is dripping seawater all over their front porch. And my dead chicken is trying to eat their welcome mat.

"Oh," says Darvish's dad as he answers the door. "It's you." He looks at the wet porch. "Did you step in a puddle? Why is my porch soaked?"

The narwhal sighs in disgust. "What does this guy want from me?" he grumbles. "I'm an ocean dweller. Next to this horn sticking out of my head, wetness is like my defining characteristic."

"Hello, Rex," says Darvish's mom. "Come on in, dear. Darvish is in his room."

"Thanks, Mrs. Darvish," I respond.

But Darvish's dad stops me. "All right. I must finally ask this question. Why do you call us that?"

"Leave the boy alone, Farooq," urges Mrs. Darvish.

"I'm just trying to understand, Sahar," he says.

"Why do I call you what, Mr. Darvish?" I ask.

"That!" he says. "You know we have a last name, Rex."

Obviously, I know Darvish and his parents have a last name. It is a good, solid Pakistani name. A name that conveys a sense of rich family heritage combined with timeless traditional values. A name that is easily lessened by overuse.

Also, I find it very difficult for me to say. Nigh impossible. I butcher it every time I try. And that's embarrassing.

But I'm not telling them that. Adults can smell fear.

"It is easy," he says. "Mestarihi. Have a go at it."

For the sake of our buddy-buddy relationship, I try. Again. "Mesh-it-tahr-ree-ree."

Darvish's dad sighs. "No, that is not correct. Are you doing this on purpose? Once more. Mestarihi."

Darvish's mom smiles. "You ignore him, Rex. You call us whatever you want."

"Thanks, Mrs. Darvish," I say, climbing the stairs to Darvish's room.

"Oh, Rex," she calls to me. "We'll be having dinner in a little bit. Would you like to join us?"

"Yippee!" crows Drumstick. "I love dinner! It's my favorite food!"

"There's food?" says the narwhal. "I could eat."

Thankfully, nobody can hear them.

"It depends," I say, following her into the kitchen. "What are you having?"

"Pancakes," she says with a smile.

"Breakfast for dinner!" says Drumstick. "Breakfast is my second-favorite food!"

"Lemme guess your third-favorite food," says the narwhal. "Lunch?"

"Nope," says Drumstick. "Tacos."

I cringe at the thought of more maple syrup. I've had my fill, thanks. I grab the fridge handle and yank the door open. "Do you have anything else? Spaghetti and meatballs, maybe?"

Mrs. Darvish smiles. "I am afraid not. There is some leftover rice pulao in there. You are welcome to anything you can find."

Darvish's dad eyeballs me from the hall. "What is wrong with you, boy?" he cries. "You go into somebody else's home and open their refrigerator? Were you raised by wild jackals?"

I confess, I don't have a good answer for this. But I have been developing a method of dealing with difficult adults. I call it the Playing Dumb Technique. I know it is a stretch for someone of my intellect, so I'm not sure if I can pull it off. But this seems like an ideal opportunity to give it a whirl.

I let my eyes glaze over. Spittle collects at the corner of my mouth. "Doi—eeeeeeeeeeee."

Darvish's dad gasps like a trout and turns to his wife. "You see, Sahar? You see what we're dealing with?"

"Relax, darling," Darvish's mom says. "He's just a boy."

Darvish's dad turns on me. "Say my last name!" he cries. "I know you can say it! I know it!"

"Calm yourself, Farooq." She pulls him to a large aquarium full of exotic fish. "Check the pH on your aquarium. That always relaxes you."

"Ooh, fish!" says the narwhal, pointing at the aquarium. "It's like they knew I was coming and put together a nice bowl of chowder for me. That right there is serious hospitality. You tell her we're staying for dinner, little man."

"Yeah!" says Drumstick, climbing into the fridge. "I think I smell an old taquito in the back here."

I grab my chicken by the wing and my narwhal by the fin, and tug them toward the stairs. Which is no small feat. When a giant sea creature gets snacky, most people swim for cover. But I am not most people.

Darvish's mom turns back to me. "Shall I set a place for you, Rex?"

"Better not, Mrs. Darvish," I say, shoving my hungry companions up the stairs. "I fell into breakfast food earlier today. It might be too soon for pancakes."

"That's no problem, dear."

"You fell into breakfast?" cries my chicken in disappointment. "I never get to fall into breakfast!"

Darvish's dad fusses with a dropper bottle at the aquarium. "He is a very strange boy, Sahar. He is just messing with us. I don't like him at all!"

It's this kind of zany banter and good-natured ribbing that defines our relationship. Like I said, Darvish's parents adore me.

8

Darvish, on the other hand, is less than thrilled to see me.

"Dude, what are you doing here?" he asks. "I told you I have homework to do."

"And I told you, more pressing matters are at hand," I remind him.

"My grades are plenty pressing," he says.

Poor chump. If only he knew how little all that book learning was going to do him out in the real world.

"This is life and death, Darvish!" I tell him. "There's a dead fish that needs our help. And his name is..." I turn to the fish in question.

"Narwhal," he answers.

"His name is Narwhal."

"Well, first," says Darvish. "That's not a name. That's a species."

"Nar...wally," I decide. "His name is Wally."

Darvish rolls his eyes. "Fine. Second, a narwhal is not a fish. It's a mammal."

I shake my head sadly at my poor deluded friend. "Mammals live on land, Darvish. Just ask any first grader. They'll tell you."

"Mammals can live in water, too!" he cries, desperate to validate the facts and figures to which he so desperately cleaves. "A narwhal is a type of whale!"

Clearly, the pressure of school is affecting his mind. I decide not to press the issue.

I sit down and soften my voice in an attempt to soothe his frayed nerves. "Darvish. You'll need to do a lot less homework and games at Iggy Graminski's house for the foreseeable future. I need you to devote your full attention to being my assistant."

"I'm not your assistant."

This kid is cute as a button. "Well, the job of sidekick has been taken by Drumstick," I tell him. "But I guess we could always revisit that decision."

"Hey!" cries Drumstick.

"I'm not your sidekick."

"Yippee!" cries Drumstick.

"Fine," I say. "We'll haggle over titles later. Right now, I need your undivided attention on this."

He pauses. And bites his lip nervously. Finally, he looks up at me. "No."

I don't like where this is going. "What do you mean, no?"

He cracks his neck. "I helped you solve the last one, Rex. I dropped everything."

The narwhal flexes his fins. "You want me to rough this guy up a little? Give him a whack with my tail? A little jab with the business end of my horn? That's usually how we handle uncooperative fish in my neighborhood."

"Stop it. Nobody's getting a jab!" I cry. I turn back to Darvish. "Look, Darvish. We are dealing with super-natural forces beyond imagining here!"

"I get that," he says. "But I have things happening in my life, too."

"Then don't do it for me, Darvish," I tell him. "Do it for Nar—Wally."

He takes a deep breath and sticks his chin out. "Fine. I'll help you."

Okay, then.

"But you're going to come to Iggy's house and play this game with me."

"What game?"

"Monsters & Mayhem!"

I eyeball my friend shrewdly. "Are you giving me an old tomato?"

"What are you talking about?" He squints at me. "I think we're having pancakes for dinner."

"Don't play dumb with me," I tell him.

"I think you mean *ultimatum*."

"That's what I said." We could save so much time if he would stop repeating me.

"Yeah," he says. "I guess I am."

"That's blackmail!" I cry. "Embezzlement! Espionage! Insider trading! I could have you impounded!"

"I don't think so," he says. He looks me square in the eyes. "You play M&M with me, and I'll help you solve your narwhal problem. That's the deal."

I sigh. The simple truth is that I need Darvish. Do not scoff. After all, some of the world's greatest minds had assistance.

Remember Sherlock Holmes? And Batman? And Ronald McDonald? I mean, what would Ronald McDonald be without that weird cheeseburger-head guy? I'll tell you what. Just a scary burger-pushing clown in yellow pajamas, that's what.

And I'm nobody's clown. So I acquiesce to Darvish's demands. "We have an accord," I say, shaking his hand.

"Darvish!" his mom calls from downstairs. "Dinner!"

"Rex!" his dad calls from downstairs. "Go home!"

"We'll start working on this tomorrow," Darvish says.

"Tomorrow?" Wally sighs. "Seriously? Jeez, you land

dwellers take forever to get stuff done. Don't you have a school of haddock that could slap this guy around? Make him see things our way? I'm telling you, guy, it's a very inefficient setup you got here."

"Relax," I tell Wally. "Just be patient and we'll have your problem figured out in no time. There's no need to rough anybody up."

"I could rough him up anyway," the narwhal suggests. "Just for funsies."

"Let's see how things go," I tell him.

"Fair enough."

"You'd better go," says Darvish. "I have to eat dinner." He opens his bedroom door. "And Saturday, you're going with me to Iggy's house."

I am equal parts annoyed and impressed with my friend. As long as I've known Darvish, he's been spineless. Moldable to my whim. Putty in my hands. If I had to pick a single word to define Darvish, it would be *spineless moldable putty.*

Just when you think you know a guy, he goes and gives you an old tomato.

9

Ms. Kincaid is our school's recess monitor. She has a sincere and upbeat attitude. She has cheerful orange hair. And her pockets are always full of Laffy Taffy. These are traits I admire in a person.

But Ms. Kincaid is a stoolie of a corrupt system. A pawn of the educational machine. A puppet of the unscrupulous establishment.

How do I know this? Because Darvish and I are trying to have an important recess meeting. We have monumental issues to sort out. Our needs demand privacy. But the jungle gym is swarming with kids. The swings play host to screaming crowds. The slides teem with an unruly mob. There is no privacy to be found here.

So we did the obvious. We tried meeting under a car in the staff parking lot. But Ms. Kincaid chased us back to the recess yard. Because hiding under a car "isn't safe."

Not to be daunted, we retreated to an abandoned shed across the street from the school. But Ms. Kincaid chastised us. Because the shed "isn't on school grounds" and is "private property."

So, nice as Ms. Kincaid is, she cannot be trusted.

Which is why we are in the dumpster behind the school.

"Why are we in a dumpster behind the school?" asks Darvish.

"Ask Ms. Kincaid next time you see her," I tell him. "But watch what you say. She's probably wearing a wire."

"This is really gross, Rex," says Darvish.

"Pay attention, man!" I say. "Your momentary

comfort is trivial compared to the matters at hand. Somebody is killing narwhals!"

"Yeah!" says Wally. "Also, I think I'm sitting in milk."

"Me too!" says Drumstick. "And it's yummy!"

"Fine," says Darvish. "What's the last thing your narwhal remembers?"

"He said something about bad water," I tell Darvish.

"That's right," says Wally. "Don't talk about it, though. It still ooks me out."

"That's it?" cries Darvish. "But what happened? How did he die?"

"I told you, it's all a blur," says the narwhal gruffly. "There I am, swimming along, minding my own business. Suddenly, there's a bright light. And a net. And lots of bubbles. I was yanked out of the water. Grubby mitts manhandling my pristine skin. And when I was put back in, there was something wrong. The water... it was bad."

Since Darvish is not as supernaturally attuned as me, he cannot hear any of this. I am forced to play go-between translator. It is slow, laborious work, but for the sake of the cause, I relay everything to my assistant.

"Bright light?" he asks. "A net? Bubbles? That could be any ocean or body of water pretty much anywhere. It's not much to go on." He shrugs helplessly. That's Darvish. Always shrugging helplessly.

I turn back to Wally. "Can't you remember anything else? Anything more specific?"

"Hey, bub!" he bristles. "I been trying to forget it! You get manhandled by humans and wrapped up in a net and see how perfectly you commit the details to memory!" He smacks Drumstick with frustration. "And you! Stop drinking old milk!"

"But it's chocolate!" protests the chicken. "I can't believe the lunch lady threw all this out!"

"Lady!" says Wally suddenly. "That's it!" The narwhal turns his javelin-tipped head back to me and Darvish. "There was somebody else there. I remember now. Just as I was starting to fade away. Just as the bad

water was working its poison into my delicate system, I saw somebody."

"Who?" I ask.

"The lady," he says. "The Iron Lady."

"The Iron Lady," I whisper.

Suddenly, the lid to the dumpster opens. I adopt a kung fu defensive stance, in case the murderer has returned to finish the job. But it's only Ms. Kincaid, the recess monitor.

"Rex?" she cries. "Darvish? I told you to stay in the recess yard. What are you doing in a dumpster?"

"Solving a crime against nature, that's what," I tell her.

"Please get out of the dumpster," she says with a smile. "I'll give you both a Laffy Taffy."

Ms. Kincaid is a very nice lady. But she doesn't give two hoots about crimes against nature.

10

It would seem that Ms. Kincaid is also a rat fink. Which is why Darvish and I find ourselves sitting outside the principal's office. Awaiting our execution.

Because that is what happens here. Obviously. I am not a troublemaker, so I wouldn't know from firsthand experience. But I have my sources. And according to my sources, roaches check in, but they don't check out.

"I can't believe you got me in trouble," says Darvish. "This is going to go on my permanent record!"

"Relax," I tell him. "You'll be dead long before then."

"What?"

"Why do you think the secretary left?" I say, pointing at Mrs. Dearhart's empty desk.

"She went to lunch," says Darvish.

"Wrong," I say. "Plausible deniability. No witnesses."

"I think she just got hungry, Rex."

"Don't be a chump, Darvish," I tell him. "One second you're innocently sitting in a dumpster. The next second you're being denied a fair trial and getting buried in an unmarked grave behind the school. This is how the world works."

"I don't think so," he says. "We'll probably just get detention."

He's a sweet kid. It makes his impending doom that much sadder.

"Come on," I say, dragging him to Mrs. Dearhart's desk.

"What are we doing!?" Darvish hisses.

"Research," I tell him, pointing at the computer keyboard. "I need you to type. I'm no good at clerical work."

You're probably wondering why I don't just have my dead chicken do all my research. After all, what's the point of having a dead chicken if he's not going to perform basic secretarial duties?

The reason is simple. That bird is never around when I need him. He is currently in my room playing Monopoly with the narwhal. Ever since Drumstick beat him at the game, Wally insists on playing until he wins. Something about "restoring the family honor."

Also, my chicken is a terrible typist. All he does is peck. It is a pathetic state of affairs.

42

"Get away from that computer," Darvish hisses, trying to pull me away. "You're going to get us in more trouble!"

"Don't be absurd," I tell him, pointing at Mrs. Dearhart's desk. "Her security measures are laughable. Do you see attack dogs? No. Do you see razor wire? No. That practically makes this a public-use machine."

"Rex!" he cries, wringing his hands.

"Pretend it's a treasure chest in your PB&J game!" I tell him.

"You mean M&M," he says.

"Whatever!" I cry. "Sneak into the dungeon and get the goodies."

He stops cold. I can see I have captured his imagination. Gone is the old tomato. Back is the putty in my hand. The world is as it should be once again.

"Fine," he says. "What am I researching?"

"Try to keep up, son," I tell him. "We need intelligence on this mysterious Iron Lady."

His fingers fly across the keyboard like tiny, agile ballet dancers. He hits Enter.

And that's when we hear it. The bells of doom. The herald of our demise. The harbinger of destruction. Mrs. Dearhart is returning from lunch. Probably with a goon squad.

By the time the secretary reaches her desk (without a goon squad...this woman knows nothing about security), we are the picture of innocence. Only we have unknowingly stolen something precious from her desk.

Knowledge. Precious knowledge.

"Well?" I whisper to my assistant. "What did the Internet have to say on the subject?"

"Margaret Thatcher," says Darvish softly. "She's known as the Iron Lady."

"Who is this Margaret Thatcher?" I ask back. "Aside from a ruthless narwhal killer?"

"She used to be the prime minister of England," he says. "Like the president. She was a very strong leader. So they called her the Iron Lady."

I knew it. This thing is international. Far-reaching. Like, England far.

It's all falling into place. "For some reason, Margaret Thatcher needed to kill a narwhal," I tell Darvish.

"Why would the former prime minister of England want to kill an ocean mammal?" asks Darvish.

"Maybe our aquatic friend knew too much," I suggest. "Maybe they had a forbidden romance. Maybe he held government secrets."

"Um..." says Darvish.

"One thing is clear," I tell him. "We're next."

"Um..." says Darvish.

"Well, the joke is on her," I say. "We'll be long dead by the time she finds us. Executed by the United States education system."

And then I hear our death knell. The principal's door opens.

Principal Wainscoat looks weary.

"Are you all right, Marjorie?" asks Mrs. Dearhart.

"Of course," says Principal Wainscoat with a forced smile. "Nothing like a twenty-minute phone call with an angry parent to start the afternoon off right."

A likely story. She probably just spent the last nine hours interrogating another student before shipping them off to a prison in Cuba. And we're next. This lady might have the wool pulled over Mrs. Dearhart's eyes, but I know how these things work.

Regardless, her weariness works in our favor.

Because she does not execute us. She does not torture us. She does not even give us detention.

She sends us back to class. And tells us to stay out of dumpsters.

Apparently, they're "not sanitary."

11

Clearly, Miss Mary has caught wind of my new bad-boy reputation. It's obvious she thinks I require supervision.

Because she is having us work on a literature project. In groups.

And she has grouped us according to desk placement. Which means I am in a group with Darvish. And Sami Mulpepper.

This just isn't going to work for me.

Why do I disapprove of being grouped with Sami Mulpepper? Is it because she smells of soup?

No. I have gotten used to this. Her brothy bouquet

is comforting at the best of times and disconcerting at the worst.

Is it because she is a straight-A student and will likely have a five-part strategy for tackling this project with gusto and verve?

No. Better her than me.

Is it because her hair catches the light in such a disarming way that it could lead to distraction and daydreaming?

Definitely not.

Then why?

The answer is simple: none of your beeswax.

Regardless of the reason, forcing me to group up with Sami Mulpepper is an outrage. It's an infringement of my civil liberties. It is a devious ploy to undermine the unmasking of a ruthless narwhal murderer.

I don't blame Miss Mary. I don't even blame Principal Wainscoat. This is above their pay grade. There can only be one person responsible.

Margaret Thatcher.

But I'm not taking this lying down. Or rather, I am.

Because, while my "group" has pulled their desks together to begin planning our project, I have chosen to hide under mine.

It's brave of me, really. Taking a stand against tyranny like this.

My brave stand comes at a cost, though. Because there are dust bunnies under here. And it seems I may have inhaled several of them.

But I'm willing to pay that price. Progress never comes without sacrifice.

12

Nobody ever thinks about Darth Vader's feelings.

How he felt when Luke blew up the Death Star. Days of planning wasted. Weeks of hard work flushed right down the space toilet. Years spent bending lesser people to your will, undone with one shot.

I understand.

It is how I feel when Darvish drops the bomb.

"Margaret Thatcher is dead."

"Dang," I say, echoing the heart's cry of Darth Vader at the moment of his undoing. I turn to the narwhal. "Don't you know what this means?"

"That your research stinks?" Wally suggests.

"No."

"That your friend over there can't type?"

"No."

"That you're gonna need a bigger bed because we're roommates forever now?"

"Definitely no," I assure him. "Think! It means that she knew we were closing in. So she offed herself before we could put all the pieces together."

Darvish shakes his head. That's just like Darvish. Always shaking his head.

"No, that's not what that means," he says.

"Of course it does, Darvish!" I cry. "Don't be a sap your whole life, man! No other explanation fits the facts."

"Except that Margaret Thatcher died years ago," he tells me. "Before any of this ever happened."

I raise my eyebrow at him. "Or did she?" This poor rube. He'll believe anything.

"Yes!" he cries. "And she didn't kill herself! She died from a stroke."

"From the stroke of her coconspirator's hand!"

"Nope," he says. "Just a normal stroke. She was an old lady."

"Oh," says Wally. "The Iron Lady I saw definitely wasn't an old lady. She looked pretty young to me."

I sigh. That's what happens when you trust a fish for your information.

You wind up killing Margaret Thatcher.

13

We are nowhere closer to discovering the narwhal's killer.

Which means a murderer runs free through the night.

Which means this poor creature's spirit is unable to move into the great beyond.

Which means I am still stuck with a giant one-horned sea creature as a bedfellow.

That's a problem for me.

So, what do you do when dark times such as these close in? Pray to the heavens above for sweet release? No. Hide your face from the world and pine for better days? Definitely not. Sink into a despair deeper than the pits of hellfire and damnation themselves? Nope.

Apparently, you play a weird board game.

"I keep telling you," says Darvish impatiently. "M&M isn't a board game. It's a role-playing game."

"I see your mouth moving, Darvish, but it's like animal noises are coming out."

"Just wait," he assures me. "You'll see."

Iggy Graminski's basement is a real dump. Sketchy. Dimly lit. Imagine a restaurant that puts lobster into their macaroni and cheese, and you'll have the essence of the place. Only with fewer forks.

It is no place for respectable citizens to gather. But when your colleagues are flattened chickens and dead narwhals, I guess you start to get less picky about the company you keep. Which is why I find myself descending into this seedy subterranean crypt with Darvish.

But before we can get all the way downstairs, I stop. Because I have heard a sound that sets my teeth on edge. It is not the rats skittering in the walls. It is not the cockroaches scuttling along the baseboards. It's worse. It is the voice of Holly Creskin.

Holly Creskin is in my class. Her favorite animal is unicorns. Her favorite color is rainbow. She is a ninny.

I halt on the stairs. "You didn't tell me Holly Creskin would be here," I whisper to Darvish.

"So what?" he says. "She's nice."

"She is a ninny," I tell him, looking up the stairs toward daylight. "Nobody has spotted us. It's not too late to make a run for it."

"No," he says. "You promised to play Monsters & Mayhem. You're playing."

As if I didn't have enough mayhem in my life.

14

Iggy Graminski sits at a table with Holly Creskin, Daniel Grimmer, and several empty chairs. The tabletop is littered with bags of chips, cans of Cherry 7UP, and assorted paper and trash. Gross. It's an outbreak of pink eye waiting to happen. I sit down and try not to touch anything.

Iggy Graminski is hiding behind a folder with a picture of a dragon on it. But his hiding skills are terrible. Because Iggy Graminski is short. But his forehead is large. Like, billboard large. You could successfully advertise car insurance on Iggy Graminski's forehead. So his forehead peeks out from behind his little screen.

"Hey, Darvish," says Iggy Graminski's forehead. "Hey, Rex."

"Are you in witness protection?" I ask his forehead.

"No," he answers.

"Is the mob hot on your trail?" I ask.

"No."

"Are you wanted for income tax evasion?"

"No."

"Then why are you hiding in your little folder fort?"

Darvish laughs. "It's his GM screen."

"Quit making up words, Darvish," I advise my friend. "It belittles us both."

"His Game Master screen," he clarifies. "He hides back there so we can't see all his maps and stuff for the dungeon he's going to lead us through."

Iggy Graminski turns to Darvish. "Maybe this wasn't a good idea."

"No, no," Darvish assures him. "It'll be fine."

"Is this where you slayed all the bung-bears last week?" I ask Darvish in whispered tones. "In this cesspool?"

"Bugbears, not bung-bears," he corrects. "And yes, it was right here."

"Well, if you see any coming, warn me," I tell him, looking at the stacks of old magazines and piles of dusty boxes that surround us. "They could be hiding anywhere in this place."

"You're a rogue," Iggy Graminski says to me.

"How dare you, scoundrel!" I say, rising from my

chair. "Is this how you welcome guests into your home? By affronting their dignity?"

Holly Creskin bursts into giggles. "No, silly! He means you're going to *play* a rogue! Like a thief or a burglar! See, I'm a warrior."

She waves at Daniel Grimmer, who sits across the table from me. "Danny is a paladin."

I have no idea what a paladin is. Something seedy, no doubt. Daniel Grimmer definitely looks the type.

"Darvish is a mage," says Holly Creskin. "And you're going to be a sneaky, conniving rogue."

Iggy Graminski hands me a paper with the word *ROGUE* across the top and a bunch of numbers. "Just one more person and we'll be all set to start."

A door slams from above. "And here comes our healer now."

Footfalls hit the basement stairs. Through the bannister, I catch the shine of tawny hair the color of sunlight on dappled leaves.

I can't believe it. I could kill Darvish. Because I am trapped in a dingy basement with my accidental girlfriend.

Sami Mulpepper.

Luckily, she hasn't spotted me. That's because I'm hiding behind Iggy Graminski's GM screen.

It's worth mentioning...his lap is not nearly as roomy as his forehead.

15

guess it's finally time to get into it. The gory details about Roadblock One: the accidental girlfriend.

Someday, when the story of my life is made into a movie, you will be able to plop down your twelve bucks and see it on the big screen with the rest of the world. But until then, I imagine there are any number of questions that must be swirling through your curious mind.

What happened at the Evening of Enchantment Dance?

Why are my waking thoughts being plagued by some torrid and unrequited (by me) love affair?

Don't I have more cosmic issues at hand that I should be free to focus upon than trivial matters of the heart?

I had hoped to spare you the shocking details. But it seems that's not in the cards. So let's get this over with.

Sami Mulpepper asked me to the Evening of Enchantment Dance. And in a moment of confusion and distraction, I said yes. I blame Darvish.

I acquired my requisite corsage. That's a flower, in case you didn't know.

I wore my requisite boutonniere. That's also a flower, in case you didn't know.

I put on my requisite tie. That's a constricting torture device that cuts off all oxygen from your windpipe, in case you didn't know.

Let the record show that we danced no slow dances. We only gyrated awkwardly when upbeat music was playing. Whenever a slow song came on, I hid in the bathroom. So you see, I never led her on.

And then it happened. The one thing that nobody, and I mean nobody, could have anticipated or foreseen.

At the end of the dance...she hugged me.

I did what any red-blooded American boy would do in similar circumstances.

I turned and ran. All the way home. Four miles. Mostly interstate.

I have avoided her diligently ever since.

But you know what a hug like that means. You, like me, understand what an embrace in a sweat-sock-scented gymnasium signifies.

The girl is obviously in love with me.

16

I have been banned from M&M. Apparently the M&M GM did not like ME invading his PS (Personal Space).

I am used to such discrimination. It comes with the territory when you are a cut above the rest. The world is not kind to the beautiful people, despite what the supermarket tabloids would have you think.

Darvish, however, is not taking it well. He stands on the curb outside Iggy Graminski's house, sulking.

As the one who vouched for my aptitude to play Monsters & Mayhem, he has been ejected from the game as well. Which, if you ask me, is a lucky break. Now he will be freed up to focus on more important matters.

He does not seem to share this optimistic outlook.

"Why couldn't you just act normal for once?" he cries.

"What was I supposed to do, Darvish?" I ask him. "You saw how Sami Mulpepper was throwing herself at me."

"She was not throwing herself at you!" he cries. "All she did was come down the stairs!" He grits his teeth in frustration. I think this game has an unhealthy hold on him. If you ask me, I've done him a huge favor.

And then I hear it. The siren call of a girl smitten by Cupid's cruel arrow.

"Rex!"

It's Sami Mulpepper. Chasing after me. I turn to Darvish with a knowing look. It's a burden being right all the time.

I turn back to Sami Mulpepper. This girl has got it bad. It's written all over her. And who can blame her, really?

I have tried to dissuade her affections. But my subtle tack has not gotten through. Uncomfortable though it is, I must set the record straight once and for all. But I vow to let her down easy.

"This has to stop, Sami Mulpepper," I tell her. "I don't love you like you love me."

She snorts. "I don't love you, Rex."

Poor thing. Her denial says more than she knows.

She squints at me. Obviously, a ploy to hold back

tears. "I was worried you had misinterpreted things. That hug didn't mean what you think it meant."

Darvish's eyes go wide. "You hugged him?"

"Hush, Darvish," I tell him. "The grown-ups are speaking."

"I was just thanking you for coming with me to the dance," Sami Mulpepper says. "That's all. You didn't have to run away."

"You ran away?" cries Darvish.

"I didn't run away," I clarify. "I had a plane to catch. Urgent matters required my immediate attention."

"Well, you don't have to keep hiding from me," she says. "Or avoiding me. I don't want things to be weird between us. I had fun."

She gives me a playful punch in the arm. Then she turns and goes back to Iggy Graminski's basement.

Leaving me on the curb. Bruised.

The bruise I'm referring to is my arm, not my heart. My heart has no cause to be bruised. None, I say. My arm on the other hand...

Well, let's just say Sami Mulpepper doesn't know her own strength.

17

I am up with the roosters the next day. Except that the only rooster I know is still asleep.

I slip from my brine-scented covers and make my weary way through the quiet house. To the breakfast table. I seek no solace beyond that which a bowl of Count Chocula can provide.

But what I find takes me aback.

It's my mother. Also known as one-half of Roadblock Five.

My mother's new job is all-consuming. Which means she is working nights and weekends. Which means I have been freed up from her well-intentioned attempts at parenting.

"Hey, buddy," she says wearily.

"Hi, Mom."

She sits in silence as I take out two bowls. Two spoons. I pour out cereal and milk for us. And I sit.

"Thanks," she says. "I think Count Chocula is just what the doctor ordered this morning."

We munch our chocolate quietly.

"I haven't seen you in a while," I tell her.

"Yeah," she says. "Sorry about that. This new job has got me burning the candle at both ends."

I can relate. Of course, being a financial advisor to a world-famous billionaire can hardly compare to the workload I face. But I don't point this out.

"Dad says he hasn't seen Darvish over in a few days," my mom comments. "Have you been hanging out at his house?"

I sigh. This is why I don't eat breakfast. It leads to gossip.

"Darvish is not speaking to me currently," I offer.

"Oh no!" my mom says with concern. "Honey, what happened?"

"It is a long and sordid affair," I tell her. "Involving bung-bears. I do not wish to discuss it. For his sake."

"Fair enough," says Mom.

I search for a new topic. Something. Anything to change the subject. To distract her weary mind. To dissuade her continued attempts to mother me.

"How's the new job?" I ask.

"I like it," she says. "My boss is a bit of a handful. And there's a lot of pressure. But I like the work. It's challenging. Fulfilling."

I seriously doubt it is as fulfilling as making key lime pies and petit fours. But I imagine it beats being an insignificant worker bee for a large financial corporation, which is what she used to do. So, for the sake of my mother, I am glad she is no longer a bee.

Of course, she cannot understand pressures like I can. The pressures of having life and death hanging in the balance.

The pressures of keeping evil and untoward figures at bay.

The pressures of watching out for my best friend, even when he is not watching out for himself.

A thought occurs to me.

My great fortitude.

My great determination.

My great unflagging spirit. Perhaps these enviable and admirable traits come to me, in some small part, from her.

Perhaps I do not give my mother enough credit.

And so, in my moment of weakness, I do something that nobody, and I mean nobody, could have foreseen.

I stand up and I give her a hug.

She grabs on and squeezes. Like a drowning man with a life preserver. Like a dog with a bone. Like a chicken with his Monopoly money.

I let her hug me.

And I hold on tight. Longer than is necessary. Because she needs it.

And for no other reason whatsoever.

That's just the kind of person I am.

18

A bleak Monday has dawned. And I have been called into a one-on-one meeting with Miss Mary.

Perhaps she wishes to gain my insight into the flaws of her teaching style. Or maybe she realizes I see through her ill-conceived scam as an imposter elementary school teacher.

Either way, I have chosen to wear something to our meeting that demonstrates my maturity and sophisticated approach to life.

A fake mustache.

"Nice mustache," she says. "Very classy."

"I thank you," I say.

Whatever else you have to say about this woman, she can appreciate a dapper 'stache. But this is not enough to win me over. I decide to put her on the defensive with a deeply probing line of questioning.

"What's with the tattoo?" I ask, pointing at the jibber-jabber on her arm. "Are those your gang colors?"

She holds out her arm. "Gosh, no. It says 'Believe in Yourself' in Polish."

I nod knowingly. "If you say so."

"You're probably wondering why I asked to meet with you, Rex," she says.

"Let's drop the pretense," I tell her. "I think we both know why we're here."

She lets out a sigh of relief. "Oh good. I appreciate your candor."

I pat her hand comfortingly. "It's good that we've acknowledged the folly of pretending."

She flashes one of her lopsided smiles. "I agree."

"So, let's get to it," I say. "Who are you working for?"

She pauses. "The school district."

I give her a knowing smile. "No. Really."

She purses her lips in concern. "Well, sometimes I work for the Tri-County Women's Wrestling Association. But that's not really why we're here."

I shake my head at her naivete. "Isn't it, though?"

She stands and begins to pace. My cool interrogation is breaking her will. It's just a matter of minutes before she tells all.

"Let's start from the beginning," she says. Here it comes. Her mysterious reason for invading our classroom. Her ulterior motive for being here. Polish tattoo, my foot. My bet is that she's a Russian spy. And then it all comes tumbling out.

"I understand you are having an issue with Sami Mulpepper being in your project group."

This is an unexpected development. I begin to take the appropriate and logical response to her line of inquiry: making a run for it. But her nervous pacing means she is blocking the door. I play for time while assessing the window-lock situation.

"Where are you getting your information?" I ask.

"Doesn't matter," she says smoothly. "The point is, I understand. I know that working closely with a girl can be nerve-racking for a boy your age."

This woman is clearly batty. But it makes sense. When they took Ms. Yardley to the nut farm, they grabbed the wrong teacher. Miss Mary was the target.

"But I'd ask you to stick it out," Miss Mary says.

"She seems super smart. When it's all said and done, I bet you'll be glad she was in your group." She sits down and clasps her hands together. But I know what she's doing. Flexing her forearms threateningly. A well-known intimidation technique.

Classic.

She flashes her lopsided smile. "What do you say?"

Play dumb. Don't let on that I recognize her manipulation for what it is. That's key.

"Sure," I say. "You bet."

"Great!" She stands and walks to the door. "I'm glad we could chat, Rex."

My mustache droops in defeat.

"And hey!" she adds, holding her door open. "I think you look really good with facial hair. You should maybe grow some mutton chops. It suits you!"

Check and mate. She's humoring me, and we both know it. It's just embarrassing.

And that's when I see it. Her fatal flaw. Her Achilles' heel. The chink in the armor. Fool! Her pride has given her away!

Because it's staring at me right there from her credenza. Among the shiny wrestling belts on display, one is emblazoned with the words that spell her doom.

Iron Lady Mid-Summer Wrestling Championship.

19

Miss Mary is the Iron Lady. That much is certain. I'm trying to explain this to Darvish, but he's being difficult.

"Get out of my room," he says moodily. "I'm not talking to you."

Which is an absurd statement. Because he obviously is. But he's still miffed about the whole M&M debacle. So I attempt to soothe him.

"Darvish! Wake up and smell the atrocities, pal!" I soothe comfortingly. "We have a ruthless assassin for a teacher!"

My friend is not convinced. Or soothed.

"You're crazy," he says.

Crazy like an ox. "She has two Marys in her name!"

I point out. "TWO! *That's* what's crazy! Those facts alone should hint at her devious nature."

He shakes his head. "That's silly. Why would Miss Mary want a narwhal dead?"

Oh, Darvish. What a cute kid. As usual, he's asking all the wrong questions.

"You mean, why would the Russians want a narwhal dead?"

"The Russians?" asks Darvish.

"Have you seen her tattoo?" I ask. "It's clearly communist in nature. She was obviously branded while training with the Russian mafia."

"The Russians aren't communist anymore," he tells me.

This guy. He knows nothing of the geopolitical climate.

"Plus, her tattoo has flowers on it," he yammers. "And butterflies."

"Clever subterfuge!" I tell him. "Designed to throw us off the trail!"

"Fine," he acquiesces. "Why would the Russians want a narwhal dead?"

"Wrong question, Darvish."

"It's the question you just asked!" he cries.

"Things move at a brisk pace in the world of international espionage," I say. "Try to keep up."

He bends over and tucks his head between his knees. "I feel light-headed."

A natural side effect of being around somebody with a dizzying intellect is that you sometimes feel left behind. Which leads to whiplash. Which leads to ODOTBS: Oxygen Deprivation of the Brain Syndrome. Everyone knows this. If Darvish was as smart as his GPA suggests, he would know to tie a pool noodle around his head to cushion him against unexpected bouts of ODOTBS. But he does not. Which is just one more mark against the educational system in this country.

I try to spell it out for him.

"The Russian secret service used Miss Mary to terminate the narwhal," I explain. "She's probably their number one fish killer."

"Narwhals aren't fish!" Darvish cries.

"Fine! *Aquatic mammal*," I concede. "Darvish, try not to interrupt me with meaningless trivia."

I'm on a roll. Any irrelevant tangent could stopper the flow of my brilliance. "Word somehow got out that we were on the trail. So they sent her in. Miss Mary. Aka the Red Wrestler. Aka Assassin Extraordinaire. Aka the Iron Lady."

Darvish is now facedown on his carpet. Which is wise, given the unsettling information engulfing him. "Why?" he says around a mouthful of carpet.

I hate to unsettle his delicate constitution further. But I'll do him no favors by hiding the grim truth. "To silence us," I tell him. "Obviously."

Darvish has gone prematurely silent.

"You're probably wondering how we handle this upsetting turn of events," I whisper calmly.

"I'm really not," he mumbles.

"The answer is simple," I tell him. "We must silence her before she silences us."

I turn to his prone form. It seems likely that he has passed out from the shock of the predicament we find ourselves in.

Which is prudent. When in doubt, pass out.

20

A day at the beach would be relaxing to many people. Those people are nitwits.

For, as I stand near Lighthouse Point, looking out onto the waters of Snarbly Bay, I know full well that these murky depths hold fathomless secrets. And dangers.

I check the bushes for Russian hitmen. It would be just like Miss Mary to send a kill crew after me. Thankfully, she currently thinks I have a mustache. So I am safe. Without it, I am just one more clean-shaven nitwit relaxing at the beach.

"This right here was one of my favorite spots," says Wally. "Good herring around here. Plus, I always like seeing the light flashing from the lighthouse."

"What's a herring?" asks Drumstick, picking his way through the rocks.

"You've never had herring?" Wally asks incredulously. "You're missing out, kid. It's only the most delectable little fish. Tastes like a blissful combo of Juicy Fruit gum and grouper. Delicious."

"What's grouper?" asks Drumstick.

"Never mind," I tell the chicken. I turn to my narwhal friend. "Why did you bring us here?"

"Yeah, why are we here?" asks Darvish, awkwardly perching on a piece of driftwood. "I don't like the sand. It's too sandy."

"You were bellyaching about needing more clues," says the narwhal gruffly. *We don't have enough details to work with. I need more clues. Whine, whine, whine. Moan, moan, moan. That's you."

"Wow, Rexxie!" crows Drumstick. "That sounded just like you!"

He sounds nothing like me. His accent is completely wrong, for a start. I hope this narwhal doesn't harbor hopes for doing voice-over work, because that dream will not turn out well.

But I don't have a chance to point this out. Because he says, "Well, I remembered something. It all happened here."

"What all happened here?" I ask.

"My traumatic capture!" Wally cries. "It all happened here. Out by that little island."

He points off the coast to a rocky shoal in the bay, covered with scrub and seagrass. A nefarious place if ever there was one.

"It's one of my favorite spots to swim," says Wally dreamily. "In the evening, the lighthouse hits the water just right. It attracts herring by the busload. I wish you could see it. Me, careening through the surf, shish-kebabbing those shiny scaled morsels right, left, and sideways. It's a thing of beauty!"

"Oh, that sounds magical," says Drumstick. "One question, though. What's a herring?"

We ignore him. "So, there I was," Wally goes on. "Enjoying the delights of an all-you-can-eat herring buffet. And this bright light hits me. I'm not gonna lie, I thought it was just the lighthouse."

"And the next thing you know, you were in a net," I finish for him.

"Exactamundo."

Darvish is dumping sand from his shoes. "You hear that, Darvish?"

"You know I can't hear them, Rex," he says grumpily.

I point to the island in question. "That's where it happened. That's where Wally was captured."

We scan the horizon. It is a desolate stretch of coast. Nothing breaks up the barren landscape of rocky dunes and beachgrass. Except one huge house, quietly overlooking the bay farther up the shore.

"What's that?" I ask, pointing at the house.

Darvish squints into the fading light. "That's Bellingham Manor."

"As in Trinity Bellingham?" I ask. "As in Dimitri Bellingham?"

"Yeah," confirms Darvish. "That's their estate."

My gears are spinning fast. My agile brain is going like a house on fire. There is probably smoke pouring from my ears at this very moment. But I couldn't care less. I only have room in my noggin for one thing right now. And that one thing is not fire safety.

It's whole-home security systems. Obviously.

"Whatcha thinking, boss man?" asks the narwhal.

"I'm thinking that a billionaire like Trinity Bellingham probably takes security very seriously," I say. "She probably has loads of security cameras protecting her plush digs."

"So?" asks Darvish.

"So," I say. "I bet some of those high-definition cameras are pointed at the bay. Right where Wally was scooped up!"

Darvish turns back to the lonely mansion towering in the distance. "How does that help us? That place is probably locked up like Fort Knox."

Some people have no imagination. It's one more reason why street smarts will beat book smarts any day.

"We need an inside source," I say.

"Doesn't your mom work for Trinity Bellingham now?" he asks.

"No good," I tell him. "She's on the payroll. We need somebody we can control. Somebody pliable."

Darvish shakes his head like the naysayer he is. "Well, we're out of luck there."

"Nay, Darvish," I tell the naysayer. "We are very much in luck."

He looks at me nervously.

"What's the plan, Rexxie?" asks Drumstick excitedly.

"Yeah. Whatcha gonna do, little man?" asks the narwhal.

"I'm going to make friends with Dimitri Bellingham, that's what."

I hope the Russian hitmen are watching. Wondering

who this mustache-less genius is. And I hope they're taking notes. Because I just outfoxed them once again.

Wally sighs sadly and stares out at the water, sparkling with the last rays of fleeting sunlight. "Well, whatever you're gonna do, do it quick-like," he says. "'Cause whoever did this is still out there. If they did it to me, they could do it to somebody else."

I put my arm around his clammy shoulder. "That's not going to happen," I tell him. "Narwhal I'm around."

"Did you just say 'Narwhal I'm around'?" groans Darvish. "Ugh. That's terrible."

But I ignore him. Because some people are too blind to see when a moment is happening right in front of their eyes. A deep, meaningful moment between a man and an aquatic mammal.

21

The True Confessions of Charlotte Doyle is considered by many to be a masterpiece of modern literature. It has won many awards. It has received praise from readers and critics alike.

I do not know who Charlotte Doyle is. Nor do I care about her blabbermouth tell-all memoirs.

Here's what I do know. I am being forced to read this book during one of the most all-consuming inquiries of my young life. It is a distraction of colossal proportions. It is a gross injustice. It is an affront to the entire marine animal community.

Clearly, the world cares more about shiny literature medals and overblown marketing hype than it does about dead narwhals.

Darvish and Sami Mulpepper insist that we must meet to work on our literature project. Sami Mulpepper suggested her house. But I said no.

Why? Because science, that's why.

When two opposing forces meet, the world could blow up. I'm paraphrasing Isaac Newton of course, but that's just basic astrology.

I am one opposing force. Sami Mulpepper is the other. So how do you stop the world from blowing up?

Meet in a neutral location.

Which explains why I am at the public library.

"Thanks for bringing brownies, Rex," says Darvish, stuffing his brownie-hole.

"Yes," says Sami. "They're really yummy."

It's not enough that I am forced spend my precious free time with an opposing force. But to add insult to injury, my dad made me bring baked goods.

I protested this ingratiating gesture. I told him it would show weakness. But he didn't care. I can see now why Isaac Newton turned his attention away from science and toward inventing the Fig Newton. Because nobody listens to scientists. But everyone listens to baked goods.

"Now!" says Sami Mulpepper. "I have to say...I really love this book! I can see why it won so many awards. Of course, Charlotte Doyle is very misguided at first..."

"But then when she rushed in to try to save Zachariah!" jumps in Darvish. "It was very dramatic."

Charlotte Doyle is not the only person who is misguided. These two have obviously been swayed by overblown hype.

"And the setting is so cool," says Sami Mulpepper. "Can you imagine being on a ship at sea in 1832? I think I would love it. The wind in your hair. The surf pounding against the ship's figurehead."

I have attempted to take Sami Mulpepper at her word when she says she does not love me. But it would be much easier if she did not insist upon inventing absurd words to impress me.

"The word is *figure eight*," I point out gently. "Not *figurehead*."

Darvish peers at me. "Rex, a figurehead is the carved figure on the front of a ship. Like a carving of a lady or a mermaid. Charlotte's ship has a seahawk figurehead."

Now she's got Darvish playing along with her ruse. My own best friend. It's a conspiracy. This is what reading uppity literature will do for you.

"Is everything all right, Rex?" asks Sami Mulpepper.

"Everything is hunky-dory," I tell her. "Why do you ask?"

"Well, after our talk, I just hoped that things would be okay between us," she says.

"Things are fine between us," I say, munching a brownie. "What makes you insinuate otherwise?"

"Because you're sitting on the floor underneath our study cubicle."

This girl thinks everything is about her. What she doesn't realize is that it's simply safer down here. Isaac Newton would have gotten hit in the head by a lot fewer apples if he had simply chosen his sitting locations more carefully.

22

I have never actually seen Dimitri Bellingham's goons
pummel anyone.

But rumors abound. Rumors of students found
stuffed into pencil sharpeners. Rumors of Middling
Falls schoolchildren fed whole to wild wolverines.
Rumors of teachers bribed to look the other way. So I
know these thugs are capable of anything.

Which makes approaching Dimitri Bellingham
difficult.

Which is why we need a distraction.

Which is why I have come up with a brilliant plan.

"Why am I dressed in a banana costume?" asks
Darvish.

"Because it's an assistant's job to perform embarrassing

but necessary tasks for their bosses," I tell him. "Speaking of, don't forget to pick up my dry cleaning after school."

"I'm not your assistant," he says. "And you're not my boss."

"Don't quibble, Darvish," I say. "Nobody likes a quibbler."

"This costume is too tight," says the quibbler. "And it smells like musty attic."

"What do you expect?" I ask. "It's my Halloween costume from first grade. It's all I could produce on short notice."

"I don't like this plan at all," he moans.

"It's simple, Darvish," I reply. "You run up to Dimitri Bellingham's bodyguards. You jab them with your cattle prod. And you run like mad out of the cafeteria."

The banana shakes his head. "I don't have a cattle prod."

"I told you to order a cattle prod. It's integral to the plan."

"I looked them up on the Internet," he says. "They cost almost a hundred dollars. I don't have a hundred dollars."

I sigh. My ideas are constantly being held at bay by the limits of my assistant's budget. "Fine," I tell him. "What do you have? A Taser? Some pepper spray? A Doberman pinscher?"

He reaches into his pocket. "I have a pencil."

It lacks pizzazz. But it will do. I am nothing if not adaptable. "Fine. Jab them with your pencil. Then run. They will give chase, and that will clear the way for me to approach Dimitri Bellingham."

"Maybe we could just go up and talk to him," Darvish suggests.

"Don't be ludicrous," I tell my friend. "Do you want to wind up stuffed into a pencil sharpener?"

"No," he says.

"Then let me do the planning, if you please."

If my best friend wound up pummeled by goons, I'd never forgive him for it. The guy doesn't always think things through, so it falls on me to look out for his well-being. I'm a good friend.

And thankfully, Darvish is a good runner, despite his cumbersome banana costume.

Because it turns out, Dimitri Bellingham's goons are faster than I have given them credit for.

23

When meeting a new friend, it's important to break the ice. Put them at ease. Ask them questions about themselves to show you are interested.

"So, Dimitri," I inquire, stepping briskly up to his table. "Tell me. What are your hobbies? Your interests? The exact number of security cameras on your property?"

"Why is your friend dressed like a banana?" asks Dimitri Bellingham, looking up from his half-eaten sandwich.

"A fair question," I say. "And the answer is simple. I have no earthly idea. Darvish is a weird kid."

I produce a rough map I have drawn of the Bellingham compound. "If you could simply mark the location of each security camera on this schematic, I'll leave you to your lukewarm grilled cheese sandwich."

"Your name is Rex, right?" asks Dimitri Bellingham.

Dang. This kid is a fortress. I crack my knuckles. I don't have time for idle chitchat. If this guy wants to play rough, I can play rough.

But I don't get a chance to begin my rigorous interrogation of Dimitri Bellingham. Because my assistant approaches, puffing like a winded water buffalo. *Sans* banana.

"Darvish, what are you doing here?" I ask. "You are supposed to be leading thugs on a merry chase disguised as a whimsical fruit."

"I gave them the slip," says Darvish.

"Is that banana-peel humor?" asks Dimitri Bellingham.

"It is," says Darvish.

"Nice," says Dimitri Bellingham.

I snap my fingers. "Darvish! Focus!"

He collapses onto the bench. "I ditched them near the boiler room and hid the costume. I wanted to meet Dimitri, too."

This gets the attention of our target. "Wait," says Dimitri Bellingham. "You guys got rid of my bodyguards so you could come meet me?"

"Yeah," says Darvish with a smile. "How come you always eat lunch alone?"

Dimitri Bellingham shakes his head in frustration. "It's these bodyguards. They scare everyone away."

"Why do you have bodyguards?" I ask. "Are you wanted by the North Koreans?"

"My mom," he says. "She's super paranoid that somebody's going to kidnap me and hold me hostage or something. Because we're so rich."

"And Principal Wainscoat is okay with them being here?" Darvish asks.

Dimitri Bellingham shrugs. "My mom donates a lot of money to the school."

I nod in understanding. The greasing of palms in exchange for lavish favors. Perhaps we can use a similar tactic to gain access to the Bellingham security tapes. I believe Darvish mentioned he has a hundred dollars.

I am about to propose this to my assistant, but he has grown distracted by something at another table.

I massage my weary temples. "Try your best to pay attention, Darvish," I say. "Staring off into space is the sign of a weak mind."

He turns back. "I'm not staring off into space." He points to a nearby table. "Iggy and Danny are looking at their *Monsters & Mayhem Adventurer's Handbook*. They're probably going to make new characters to replace ours."

This gets Dimitri Bellingham's attention. "You guys play Monsters & Mayhem?" he asks excitedly.

"Did," says Darvish, shooting me a sour look.

"Darvish got kicked out of his M&M group," I explain. "It preys on his mind."

"*I* got kicked out?" he cries indignantly. "*You* got me kicked out!"

Dimitri Bellingham would have no way of knowing the wound he just opened. But a true friend like me can see the pain. The poor guy is still bitter about his recent spate of bad luck.

Dimitri Bellingham moves his lunch tray aside. "I LOVE M&M!" he cries. "I just never have a group to play with. But I have all the rule books! I read them all the time. They're practically memorized."

I would expect a man of Dimitri Bellingham's means to have more exotic pursuits. Mountaineering. Dogsledding. Porpoising through a money bin full of cash like Scrooge McDuck. But no. He's just as big of a dork as Darvish.

"And I have a huge collection of painted Monsters & Mayhem miniatures!" cried Dimitri Bellingham.

Darvish gasps in addle-brained excitement. "You paint M&M minis?"

I smile to myself. Because, thanks to my careful engineering, another door of opportunity has opened. And this door could give us access to Bellingham Manor's surveillance system.

Darvish is a role player. Iggy Graminski is a role

player. Even Dimitri Bellingham, it would seem, is a role player. I am not a role player. I am a straight-shooting man of the streets.

But for the sake of the animals, I reach deep and disguise myself in a cloak of enthusiasm as believable as any banana costume.

"Monsters & Mayhem miniatures?" I cry excitedly. "Now, that is a collection I would love to see! In person! And immediately, if not sooner!"

24

Spy drones. Pit bulls. Electrified fences.

These are the kinds of things I respect.

And Bellingham Manor has them in abundance.

Which means Trinity Bellingham takes security seriously.

Which means Trinity Bellingham is hiding something.

But what? Has she amassed her riches through nefarious means? Is she in the pocket of a foreign government, sent here to undermine our democracy? Is she running an illegal steroid smuggling ring?

None of this is my concern. I don't judge the ethical failings of others. As long as she is not involved with the likes of Margaret Thatcher and Mary-Kate Mary, she's okay by me.

It is easy to turn a blind eye to any legally ambiguous activities when you are reaping the rewards of a newfound friendship with her son. Which currently involves me sitting in an electric massaging chair. Drinking chocolate Nesquik. And eating strawberry bonbons.

Dimitri Bellingham's Monsters & Mayhem collection is housed in its own building on the Bellingham compound. It's just a little playhouse. Like a tree fort, roughly twice the size of my entire home.

Darvish is in a rapturous state of bliss. "This is the coolest collection of M&M minis I've ever seen!" he screeches. "You have rangers. You have paladins. You have everything!"

"Thanks," says Dimitri. "It's nice to have somebody to show them to." He turns to me. "You guys should come over and paint minis sometime. It would be fun!"

Dimitri Bellingham is a really nice guy. Which makes him easy to manipulate. Which I almost feel bad about doing. Until I remember . . . it's for the animals.

"You know what else would be fun?" I tell him. "Looking at your mom's security footage. Footage of the last two weeks from cameras that point exactly south-southwest of here toward the ocean would be especially fun. As an example."

He gives me a funny look. "That's a very odd and specific request."

I shrug. "What can I say? I'm a camera nerd."

"Oh," says Dimitri Bellingham, nodding. "Okay."

This kid is lapping up every spoonful I feed him. I'm starting to see why Iggy Graminski cast me as a rogue. I've got this sneaky, conniving thing down to a science.

But then Dimitri Bellingham lays it on me. Bad news. The kind of bad news that makes grown men weep and grown dogs howl at the moon. The kind of bad news that nobody, and I mean nobody, could have seen coming.

"The thing is, I'm not allowed in the security room," says Dimitri Bellingham.

This guy is quickly proving himself useless.

Lucky for him, I really like this massage chair. Otherwise, I would be so out of here by now.

25

Man cannot live on bonbons and Nesquik alone. He needs free rein. He needs carte blanche. He needs the freedom to wander the expansive grounds of the Bellingham estate and look for clues.

Luckily, Dimitri Bellingham may have redeemed himself on that score.

Because, seeing my disappointment about the security room, he has suggested we go to the kitchen instead.

"Do you guys like key lime pie?" he asks. "The cook just made some!"

I sigh. It's not the complete and full access to every secret nook and private cranny of his home that I was hoping this brand-new relationship would grant me.

But it is key lime pie. My favorite type of pie. It's a step in the right direction.

"Darvish," I hiss. "Keep your eyes peeled."

"What am I looking for?" he whispers back.

"Isn't it obvious?" I tell him. "I don't know! But this house has a perfect view of the spot where Wally got nabbed. Perhaps the grounds crew saw something. You question them while I keep Dimitri busy."

"I'm not doing that," says Darvish.

I shake my head in frustration. Putty-in-my-hand Darvish seems to be swerving back toward old-tomato Darvish. And his timing could not be worse.

"Well, at least keep your eyes peeled for secret doors," I insist. "They could lead to the security room."

"And what am I supposed to do if I find one?" he asks.

Poor Darvish. No gumption. He needs instructions for every little thing.

"You are to fashion some sort of rudimentary lock-picking device. Gain entry and quickly peruse all the footage from around the time of the narwhal's death."

"Um..." says Darvish.

Dimitri Bellingham leads us up the lavish front steps to the main house. Ten-foot-tall doors tower over us, embellished with gold. The gaudy trappings of the rich. I make a mental note to acquire some gaudy trappings of my own as soon as humanly possible.

But when the doors open, I see something that makes my stomach turn. More than Darvish's old tomato. More than week-old key lime pie.

I see heads. The walls are covered with them.

Dozens of animal heads.

Dead animal heads.

26

When examining the cruel underbelly of the criminal world, one must turn over many rocks. And slimy things live under rocks. Disturbing things. Things it's not polite to talk about in civilized society.

Slugs.

Worms.

Disembodied animal heads lining the walls of a billionaire's mansion.

We never made it to the kitchen. The great grandfather clock in Dimitri Bellingham's parlor chimed out the five o'clock hour. And Darvish said he had to go home for dinner.

Which is why I didn't find any secret doors.

Which is why I failed to question the landscaping staff.

Which is why I never got pie.

Dinner always messes everything up.

I offered to accompany Darvish. But he said he had homework to do. He said he needed some alone time.

Darvish doesn't fool me. We've been friends for too long. I know that "I have homework to do" and "I need some alone time" are just code words for "I need my best friend and his dead chicken and his dead narwhal close beside me."

So that is where we are.

Dinner consumed, homework complete, the guy should be a bundle of joy right now.

And yet, he is not.

Poor Darvish. Perhaps the day's events have taken their toll. Perhaps the pressure is getting to be too much. Perhaps the sight of the Bellingham Hall of Horrific Heads has left him on the emotional brink.

Because he is now standing in front of his dad's aquarium. Staring vacantly at the fishies. A broken man.

"I'm not a broken man," he tries to convince me. But I know better. We all do.

"Uh-oh," says Drumstick. "This reminds me of a cardinal friend of mine. He flew straight into a closed window. From that day on, he thought he was a duck. Just

101

went around quacking all day long. Just quack-quack-quack. That's all we could get out of him. We had to put him in a home."

"Yeah, I think your pal is suffering some sort of emotional trauma," says Wally. "I've seen it before. It ain't pretty."

I agree. But we must be gentle.

"Snap out of it, Darvish!" I say, trying to coax him from his stupor. "We don't have time for your nervous breakdown right now."

"I'm not having a nervous breakdown," he says.

Strong little man. Trying to put on a brave face.

"I know all the heads upset you," I tell him, the model of understanding. "They would upset anyone with a delicate constitution."

He rolls his eyes. "I'm not upset about all those heads. And I don't have a delicate constitution."

"Then what's wrong?" I ask.

"I don't know. It's been a rough week. And seeing Dimitri's minis made me think...I just really miss playing M&M with my group."

I tsk in his general direction. I knew this game was trouble.

It all makes sense. The streak of independence. The old tomato. The mood swings. It's this game. This world of paladins and bung-bears is wreaking havoc on his impressionable young mind. This flight of fantasy is gumming up the works. This gang of role-playing riff-raff is interfering with the well-oiled dynamics of our friendship.

The sooner we solve this narwhal situation, the sooner I can get Darvish back to his normal, moldable self.

He pulls a number of bottles and vials out of the aquarium cabinet. "My dad says checking the pH of his fish tank relaxes him. Maybe that would be a good hobby for me. Since I can't play M&M anymore."

"Darvish. Pal. Buddy," I say, trying to refocus him on the important matters at hand. "You don't have time for hobbies. Supernatural world-shattering things that defy everything we know about death and the afterlife are in the works. And you get to be a part of it!"

"Sure," he says, scooping aquarium water into a vial and shaking it. "I guess I should be happy that I can't play my favorite game anymore."

"That's the spirit. Now put that slightly unhinged mind to work and think!" I tell him. "Why does Trinity Bellingham have a wall full of dead animal heads?"

He stops shaking his vial. "Oh, that's easy," he says. "Not only is Trinity Bellingham a billionaire. She's also a big-shot hunter."

"What?" I wheel around and point a skeptical finger at him. "Where are you getting this information?"

He shrugs. "I looked her up on the Internet."

"You broke into the school office and accessed Mrs. Dearhart's computer?" I cry, gasping with incredulity. "In your fragile condition?"

"It's not the only computer in the world, you know," he informs me. "I used my laptop."

"Did you scrub it first?" I ask. "It could be hacked. That thing could be crawling with viruses and malware."

Darvish goes on. "Trinity Bellingham travels all over the world to hunt animals. Legally. She's pretty famous. They call her the Flaming Hunter of the West."

"That's a weird name," I say. "Why do they call her that?"

"Was she burned in a fire?" asks Drumstick.

"Is this lady a pyromaniac?" asks Wally.

"Does she really love s'mores?" asks Drumstick. "Because you know who really loves s'mores? Me."

"It's because she has flaming orange hair," says Darvish.

And then it hits me. A flash so brilliant, I'm surprised everyone in the room is not blinded.

"Wait a second!" I say. "You know who also has flaming orange hair?"

"Who?"

This kid wants to know who. It goes to show just how far gone he is. For there is one person who has attempted to thwart us time and time again, to no avail. One person who has shown themselves to be duplicitous and untrustworthy. One person who has no respect for the concerns of animals nor the God-given rights of every young person to sit and chat in a garbage dumpster.

"Ms. Kincaid!" I cry. "That's who!"

Darvish shakes his head wearily and peers at the vial. "Eight point four. Perfect pH." He sighs. "My dad was right. This is relaxing."

"Hush, child." I pull Darvish's head to my chest. And I pat it like a petting zoo llama.

"Oh, that's nice," he says. "Thanks, Rex."

What can I say? A broken man deserves some comfort as the last vestiges of sanity leave him.

27

There is an upside to having a two-faced trickster as a teacher.

She is probably so consumed with her Machiavellian shenanigans that she won't notice the difference between my handwriting and chicken scratchings.

Which is the perfect opportunity to put Drumstick's free time toward something more useful than playing Monopoly with a narwhal.

He has proven useless at math homework. So I give him something more suited to his creative bent. My literature project.

With him reading *The True Confessions of Charlotte Doyle* and tackling all the subsequent busywork, I will be freed up to focus on more important issues.

Assuming my chicken can read, I have no reason to believe this won't turn out well.

His greatest challenge will be finding uninterrupted time. You would think this would be a nonissue when you are a dead chicken with the endless span of infinity at your disposal.

But no. Because Wally is monopolizing all of Drumstick's leisure hours. Literally.

This narwhal is obsessed with defeating my chicken at a board game. He challenges the bird at every available moment. According to Wally, the honor of generations of narwhals hangs in the balance.

I suggested they try something besides Monopoly. I will keep future suggestions like this to myself.

Because Uno was an unmitigated disaster.

Risk was a complete catastrophe.

And his performance during Battleship was just embarrassing. You would think he would have done better in a seafaring game. But no.

And so he is now back to Monopoly, more committed than ever to achieve victory.

I'm telling you, ever since this narwhal came on the scene, the order of my universe has gone wonky. Everyone I know has GPDs (Game Preoccupation Disorders).

Darvish is suffering an acute case of PMMA (Post Monsters & Mayhem Angst). Drumstick has been ravaged by MIML (Monopoly Is My Life).

I like Wally. He's the nicest narwhal I've ever known. But I'm ready for him to win his ticket to paradise. Then maybe, just maybe, everyone can return their focus back to where it belongs. On me.

The narwhal in question cackles maniacally. "I've got you now, birdbrain!" Cleverly, he has adopted a new three-pronged strategy.

He has started putting all the hotels in his mouth.

He has begun wearing the tiny top hat on his head.

And he insists that Drumstick call him "Guido" during all game play. He says it's his gamer tag. I suspect it is simply a ploy to establish dominance over the bird.

I hope he wins a game soon. Because I think it's starting to affect his emotional stability.

Also, I'm running out of board games.

28

I am invisible.

I am stealthy.

I am one with a recycling bin.

That's because it is recess. And I am tailing the felonious Ms. Kincaid. Aka Trinity Bellingham. Aka the Flaming Hunter of the West.

My theory is brilliant in its simplicity:

1. Trinity Bellingham has a wall full of heads.
2. As a known killer of animals, she has been added as a prime suspect in the death of our narwhal.
3. Trinity Bellingham has flaming orange hair.
4. So does Ms. Kincaid.

Ergo...Trinity Bellingham, eccentric billionaire and world-famous hunter, IS Ms. Kincaid, humble recess monitor. In disguise.

Why? you may ask. Why is a filthy rich weirdo lurking around my school in such a transparent ruse?

The answer is obvious to anyone with half a brain: I have no earthly idea. But she is. The orange hair is a clear giveaway.

Now I just have to prove it.

Which is why I am invisible.

And stealthy.

And one with a recycling bin.

Which is exactly when Darvish blows my cover.

"Why are you wearing a fake mustache?" he asks.

"SHHH!" I hiss, yanking him behind the bin with me. "Miss Mary thinks I've grown facial hair. I have to keep up the charade when I'm on her turf."

"Oh," he says. "Why are you hiding behind a recycling bin?"

"I'm conducting surveillance on Ms. Kincaid!"

"What?" he cries. "I thought you were joking about that."

Darvish is my very best friend. As such, he should know full well that I never joke about surveillance.

"Ms. Kincaid is not Trinity Bellingham in disguise," he says.

"And how do you know that?" I ask accusingly.

"Because I saw a picture of Dimitri's mom on the Internet," he tells me. "And she looks nothing like Ms. Kincaid."

I must admit . . . recess is almost over, and I have yet to witness any suspicious activities. Ms. Kincaid has blown her whistle four times. She has given two children Laffy Taffy. And when a stray dog ran onto the playground, she simply chased the dog away, rather than trying to mount its head upon her wall.

It is very disappointing. I turn to Darvish. "Where have you been?"

"Talking to Iggy and Danny," he says. "I asked them if I could come back to M&M."

"What did they say?" I inquire.

Darvish raises an eyebrow at me. "Iggy said I could come back only if you apologize to him."

My jaw flies open at the affrontery. "For what?" I cry.

"Rex," he sighs. "You jumped in his lap, flipped the table over, and threw his GM screen at Sami."

Any fool could see that those acts were done in self-defense. I'm about to tell this to Darvish. But instead, I grab him and jump into the recycling bin.

"Silence!" I cry, removing a root beer can from my hair. "The suspect approaches!"

But as the lid to the recycling bin opens, I see the

111

truth of Darvish's words. There is no ruthlessness or cunning is Ms. Kincaid's eyes as she peers down at us. Only heartfelt confusion.

"Fellas?" she says. "What is it with you and trash cans?"

29

I am trying diligently to put two and two together. I am working tirelessly to fit the puzzle pieces into place. It's difficult to do when you are surrounded by slack-jawed layabouts.

Drumstick is playing *Sandy Smush* on my dad's phone. It is a game involving squashing little beach-combing crabs into jelly. It is repetitive and tiresome and a colossal waste of his valuable time. But he is a dead chicken. So I leave him to his amusements.

Wally is on the Internet watching Monopoly tutorials. His incessant mouse clicking is irritating and mind-numbing and could drive a person stark raving mad. But he has a family debt of honor to avenge. So I do not impede his progress.

Darvish is in my beanbag chair, peacefully reading a book. Which is not just a waste of time. Which is not just mind-numbing. It is a slap in the face of the entire animal kingdom. It is an affront to the many fitful hours I have invested in this mystery. And it is, let's be honest, the opposite of contributing.

I can no longer hold my tongue. "Darvish, would you say you are for or against marine life?"

"Um...for," he says without looking up.

"Do you want a ruthless murderer to strike once more against the heart of the sea?" I ask pointedly.

"I don't think so," he says.

"Then, in the name of sweet Hercules, what are you doing?" I cry.

"I'm reading *The True Confessions of Charlotte Doyle*," he says, lowering the book. "It's really good. I don't want to get a bad grade on this project because of you."

"I suggest you get your priorities in order, Darvish," I tell him. "Solving murders, first. Pointless leisure activities, second."

"This isn't a pointless leisure activity," he says. "It's one-third of our English grade. The real question is: Why aren't *you* reading *The True Confessions of Charlotte Doyle*?"

"Rest assured," I tell him. "My best people are working on it."

"On it, boss!" cries Drumstick, smushing another sandy crab mercilessly.

"Now *focus!*" I say to Darvish. "We know Ms. Kincaid is just a patsy. She's too naive to be wrapped up in the underworld of oceanic assassination."

"That's what I said," Darvish points out.

"We know Miss Mary is the Iron Lady," I muse. "She was the last person who Wally saw before he faded into oblivion."

"If you say so," says Darvish.

"But we also know Trinity Bellingham has a wall full of animal heads."

"Which is disturbing," says Darvish.

"Oh my gosh!" I cry with realization. "That's it! The Russians have nothing to do with it!"

"What are you talking about?" he asks.

"Her name, Darvish!" I cry.

"Trinity?"

"Make an effort, man!" I yell, grabbing him by the scruff of his collar. "BELLINGHAM!"

"What about it?"

"It's vaguely European!"

"Is it? So what?"

"Miss Mary has a Polish tattoo!" I point out.

"So?" Darvish asks.

"Poland is in Europe!" I shout to the heavens. "Don't

you see the connection? They're in cahoots! Where do you think Miss Mary is getting all those golden belt buckles?"

"From winning wrestling matches."

I rub my eyes. It's like I'm working with a house cat.

"She's being paid off, Darvish!" I tell him. "It all makes sense! Miss Mary is Trinity Bellingham's dead-animal supplier!"

"I don't know," says Darvish skeptically. I swear. The glass is always half broken with this guy. "Did you see any narwhal heads on the wall?" he asks. "That might convince me."

Of course. The narwhal head is the smoking gun. At long last, the kid is contributing.

"Wait just a minute," says Wally. "You think my beautiful mug might be hanging up on that lady's wall someplace?" His ghost mist turns greener than normal. "That is disgusting."

Disgusting, yes. But also proof positive. We find it on the wall of Bellingham Manor, and we've got Miss Mary and Trinity Bellingham in flagrante delicto.

Which is an industry term that means "with a narwhal on her wall."

30

There are many important life lessons to be garnered from the *Indiana Jones* movie franchise.

Always carry a bullwhip. Don't make a fourth movie. And most important: Just when you've made a breakthrough, that's usually when you suffer a humiliating setback.

Well, just as I feel we're closing in on our prize, there's a knock on my bedroom door.

The humiliating setback has arrived. And it comes in the form of my dad.

I'm not sure why he bothers knocking. Because every knock is immediately followed by him barging in. You'd think he owns the place.

"Sorry to interrupt, Rexxie," my dad says. "But your

mom has some fancy shindig for work. And we've been invited."

"Please give my regrets, Dad," I tell him. "I have bigger fish to fry."

"Technically an aquatic mammal," chimes in Darvish helpfully.

I nod. "Exactly."

"Sorry, pal," my dad says with a shrug. "I know you've got a lot going on with school. But we're going to this party. It'll impress Mom's new boss if we make an appearance."

I shake my head toward the heavens. The assumptions people make simply because they gave birth to you. It's honestly astounding.

"I do not have time for workplace politics!" I cry. "Darvish and I have just had a huge breakthrough in our...literature project! I cannot spare the time to attend some prance-about soiree!"

"Well, I don't know how much prancing you're going to do," he says. "But it is pretty ritzy. We'll need to rent tuxedos."

"A tuxedo?" cries Wally. "Well, la-dee-dah!"

"Yeah," chimes in Drumstick. "I didn't know there was a dress code around here or I would have worn my fancy feathers!"

They bust into ghostly laughter. I shoot them a dirty look, which is about all I can do with my dad in the room.

My dad unfurls a red measuring tape and wraps it around my chest. "So, I need to get your measurements."

"Dad!" I cry. "This invasion of my personal space is completely unwarranted. I can tell you my measurements. I am a boy's medium."

My dad chuckles and encircles my throat with his measuring tape like an assassin's garrote.

"Sorry, bub," he says unremorsefully. "I need a little more than that. And it'll go much quicker if you stop squirming."

"Father!" I cry. "I demand you stop manhandling me in front of my entourage!"

He ignores me and reaches down to embarrassingly measure my inseam. "I think you need a few more people than Darvish if you're going to have a proper entourage," he says. "No offense, Darvish."

"None taken, Mr. Dexter," says Darvish, enjoying my misery.

"And, guys..." My dad reaches over and yanks open a window. "Air this place out, would you? I get that being a sixth-grade boy comes with its own special set of smells, but it stinks like week-old fish sticks in here."

He closes the door behind him. Leaving me with a laughing narwhal, a giggling chicken, a snorting best friend, a twenty-nine-inch inseam, and a deep burning desire for my very own bullwhip.

31

I set down my tray of meat loaf with the kind of decisive slam that shows the world my get-it-done attitude and my disdain of school lunches all in one bold gesture.

"Let's do this, Darvish," I tell my friend.

He looks up from his lunch. "What are we doing?" asks Darvish.

"Reconnaissance," I tell him. "Pretend it's a quest in your BLT game."

"BLT?" He shakes his head. "You mean M&M."

"They're both foods, Darvish!" I tell him. "Picture it. We shall enter the lion's den. We shall breach the dragon's lair. We shall infiltrate the source of ultimate evil. And this time we shall find what dwells within!"

"I still don't know what any of that means," says Darvish.

"La pomme!" I cry, trying to break through. "El toreador! Maserati!"

Darvish just stares at me.

I get it. My mind races at breakneck speed. Keeping up is difficult for the intellectual rank and file. I try to use small words.

"We. Search. Narwhal. Head."

Understanding registers. "Back to the Bellinghams'?"

"Yes!" I cry, waving my arms about. "Today! Before our teacher-in-wolf's-clothing strikes again!"

"Why didn't you just say that?" he cries.

"I did!" I tell him. "In four languages!"

"Gosh, I don't know," moans Darvish, wringing his hands.

"What's wrong with you?" I ask. "You didn't eat the meat loaf, did you? Darvish, I've told you a hundred times ... don't eat the meat loaf."

"No, it's not that," he says uneasily. "It's just ..."

"You're scared of the animal heads," I deduce.

"Well, they are kind of gross," he says. "But it's not that. It's just ..."

"Spit it out, Darvish."

He looks across the cafeteria at Dimitri Bellingham's table. "I don't like using Dimitri like this. He's a really nice guy."

"We're not using him!" I cry indignantly.

"It kind of feels like we're using him."

I take a seat and drape an arm around his shoulder. "Buddy. Pal. Compadre. Do you like this kid?" I ask.

"Yeah, I do!" he says. "We're interested in some of the same things."

"Do you authentically enjoy his company?" I inquire.

"Yes!" he exclaims. "I can't believe we never hung out with him before."

"Then let your conscience rest easy," I say. "We're not using anybody."

"We're not?" Darvish asks.

"Of course not," I tell him. "We are befriending a lonely boy at a time and place that happens to offer us ample surveillance opportunity. It's a win-win."

Darvish has no response. I take his silence as an acknowledgement of my wisdom. And I drag him toward Dimitri Bellingham.

The goon squad bristles at our approach, but Dimitri Bellingham snaps his fingers and they heel.

"Hey, Dimitri!" I say. "What's going on?"

"Just reading *The True Confessions of Charlotte Doyle*," he says, holding up his book. "Have you read this thing? It's really dramatic."

The author of this book should give his marketing people a big fat raise.

"I'm vaguely familiar with the title," I say. "What do you say we hang out at your place after school? Paint some minis."

"Yeah!" interjects Darvish.

"Maybe this time you can give us the grand tour of your rad pad," I add. Which is modern urban slang for "show us around your house."

"Why are you talking like that?" Darvish asks me.

"This is how I always talk," I assure him. "I'm a man of the people."

"Gee, guys, I can't," says Dimitri Bellingham. "My mom's got some business meetings happening at the house over the next couple days. She won't want anybody around. How about later this week?"

Darvish nods. "Yeah, that sounds great!"

The bell rings. We turn to go.

"And, guys," Dimitri Bellingham calls, "you don't have to be afraid of Aldo and Sidharth." He motions to his bodyguards. "You can come eat lunch with me anytime."

"Okay," says Darvish. "Sounds good."

We head to class. "See?" Darvish points out. "He's nice."

I sigh. "I'll admit, he is nice. You know what would be even nicer?"

"What?"

"If he sweetened the deal with the guarantee of key lime pie," I say.

It's just a fact of nature. Key lime pie makes every nice thing just a little bit nicer.

32

This literature project is quickly becoming the bane of my existence.

It's all Miss Mary will talk about. When we bust her for her felonious activities, I'm going to make sure my lawyers tack on a civil suit for impinging upon my personal well-being. Her so-called literature project may be causing me lasting pain and suffering.

"So," she chirps from her desk. "Does anybody have any final questions about the literature project before we move on to other things?"

Sami Mulpepper raises her hand. "What if you are having a small problem in your group?"

"What type of problem?" asks Miss Mary.

"Like, what if somebody isn't doing their share of the work?"

Ah. I see what's happening here. Sami Mulpepper is feeling guilty because I am doing all the heavy lifting. I see her point. To date, she has brought zero plates of brownies to our work sessions. As much as I hate to admit it, I must agree with her. This imbalance of work distribution must stop.

Miss Mary rises and paces the front of the room. "That's a great question, Sami." She looks out over the class. "It would be my hope that each member of every group is pulling their own weight."

"But what if one person isn't?" asks Sami Mulpepper.

It's an inane question. The answer is obvious. That person should stop by a good bakery before her next work session. Problem solved.

"Well, if you can't find a balance that works for everybody, you can come talk to me after school sometime," my teacher says. "But I can't stay today. I have a wrestling match this afternoon."

The room fills with excited titters. "That's so cool!" says Holly Creskin. "Are you excited?"

"I am," says Miss Mary with a lopsided grin. "But I'm available to you after school any other day this week. However, I encourage everybody to do their fair share of work in these groups. I think you'll agree I'm very easygoing. But I won't tolerate any guff. Okay?"

Guff? Guff? Who says *guff*?

It's as plain as the mustache on my face.

The kind of person who was trained by Cold War–era KGB, that's who.

The kind of person who can net a narwhal at six hundred feet, that's who.

The kind of person who will probably side with students who eat brownies but don't make them.

That's who.

33

It would seem this day is destined to be filled with guff.

Guff like Ms. Kincaid watching me like a hawk at recess. Which is a violation of my privacy and my right to sit in a garbage can if I so choose.

Guff like Beefarooni being served at lunch today. Which everyone knows gives you the Beefarooni sweats.

Guff like being dragged to the Riddle-Me-This Hobby Shop by Darvish. Which is where I am now.

"Explain to me one more time why we're here?" inquires Wally.

"The narwhal asks a valid question," I tell Darvish.

Per usual, Darvish has his nose stuffed in a book.

But he withdraws his snoot long enough to shoot me a look of disdain. "You know I can't hear them."

"Right. Allow me to translate. Why are we here?"

He huffs in exasperation. That's just like Darvish. Always huffing in exasperation. "I don't understand why we can't do something that I want to do for five minutes," he says, holding up the book he's perusing. "I told you. I want to pick up my own copy of the *Official Monsters & Mayhem Creature Compendium*."

I shake my head sadly. "Oh, Darvish. That again? Let's move on. You know you're not allowed to play that game anymore. You got kicked out."

He slams the book closed and shoots me a look. "You are unbelievable."

Poor guy. I can see that this case is taking its toll on him. I speak slowly and softly, gently tapping the brakes of his emotional roller coaster. The last thing we need is for Darvish to snap again.

"Darvish," I explain gently. "Have you considered the possibility that you do not play well with others? Maybe people are starting to take notice. And now it has affected your participation in certain social circles. Perhaps it's for the best."

"I don't play well with others?!" he shouts. *"Me?"*

We can never see our own shortcomings. It is the tragedy of the human condition. Darvish cannot help that he is not a team player. But he is my friend. And I accept him as he is, regardless of his many flaws.

"Hey, kid!" yells the hobby-shop guy. "Did you come here straight from the pool?"

I do not follow his meaning. Perhaps this is another one of those M&M code words. I do my best to speak his native tongue. "I am a rogue."

"I don't care what you are," he says, pointing at the soggy carpeting behind me. "You're making a puddle on my rug! Get out of here!"

"It's discrimination, that's what it is," grouses the narwhal. "*We don't serve wet things. We don't serve briny things. We don't serve things with only one horn.*" He heads toward the door. "Let's get outta this dump before I lose my temper."

"We will leave, shopkeep," I tell the hobby-shop guy. "But know this! You have lost my business! Come along, Darvish!"

"No," says Darvish grumpily. "I think I've had enough."

"What are you talking about, Darvish?" I ask patiently.

He shelves his book and stares at me. Silence hangs between us like a wrecking ball.

"I'm not so sure we should hang out anymore," he finally says.

"Come on, Darvish—" I begin.

"No," he interrupts. "You got me kicked out of my M&M group. You won't apologize to Iggy. I don't even think you care."

I sigh. "There, there, Darvish," I tell him wearily. "You just have low blood sugar. Let's get an Orangina. You'll feel worlds better."

"No," he says solemnly. "I'll help you with this narwhal thing. I said I would. But after that? Well...I don't know, Rex."

"Let's go, kid!" the unreasonable shopkeeper berates me.

"You should go," says Darvish. He pulls his *Creature Compendium* from the shelf once again. "And I do play well with others," he mutters. "You just can't see it."

I see everything. And Darvish sees nothing. Not because he won't. Because he can't.

He can't see that what we are up against is bigger than the two of us.

He can't see that ever since this narwhal has come into my life, Darvish has slipped further out of it.

And he can't see what nobody, and I mean nobody, could have foreseen.

That I'm scared.

Not scared of an oceanic assassination conspiracy that could stretch across the reaches of the European continent. Not scared of Miss Mary and her intimidating physique and her wily ways. Not scared of a loudmouthed hobby-shop storekeeper who most assuredly lives in his mother's garage.

No. I'm scared that . . .

That in the not-too-distant future, Darvish and his new best friends Iggy Graminski and Daniel Grimmer and Holly Creskin are going to be sitting in Iggy's basement playing M&M every day after school.

And I'm going to be sitting around with a dead narwhal and a dead chicken that nobody can see.

Alone.

I turn slowly toward the door. And that's when I see her. Somebody that fills me with horror. And dread. And regret that I'm not wearing a raincoat.

"Yo! Yo!" she says. "What's up, fishes?!"

There's one other thing Darvish can't see. The dead whale shark standing there in the Riddle-Me-This Hobby Shop.

Dripping seawater all over me.

34

Darvish has abandoned me. It is a nightmare.

I am a Sherlock without a Watson. A Batman without an Alfred. I'm like Ronald McDonald before he met all those other weirdos, back when he was just selling McNuggets out of the back of a van.

And yet. I muddle on. Because, in spite of my abandonment, the appearance of this dead whale shark has done more than just doubled my workload and multiplied the malodorous stench in my room.

She has brought a revelation. And that revelation is that my teacher is not just a killer of large aquatic wildlife. She is also a liar.

"I've been an fool!" I cry, pacing my bedroom. "A booby! A buffoon!"

The whale shark scratches her head with an enormous fin. "Sheesh, bro. If you're the guy who's supposed to help me, you're not exactly filling me with, like, confidence right now. For serious."

"Wow," says Drumstick. "That is one big fish."

The chicken's not lying. This creature towers above us, shrouding us in a pool of green mist. It doesn't seem possible that she can actually fit into my bedroom. And yet, here she is, dribbling water all over my bedsheets.

"Big and beautiful," says the whale shark. "I had this squid friend, mkay? He used to call me Grande Bonita. That was before I accidentally ate him."

"You ate your friend?" asks Drumstick in horror.

"It was an accident, mkay?" she says. "I was always like, don't get between me and my lunch, Paco." She shakes her enormous head sadly. "Paco didn't listen."

Drumstick turns back to me. "You were saying you're a booby," he reminds me. "Why are you a booby exactly?"

"I was taken in, Drumstick!" I tell him. "I know where Miss Mary spent her afternoon!"

"She had a wrestling match," the chicken reminds me. "That's what you said."

"Lies!" I cry. "Nonsense! Bull hockey! She didn't have a wrestling match! And Trinity Bellingham didn't have a business meeting!" I yank my finger at the enormous fish crowding my personal space. "They were bumping off another sea creature!"

"Yo. Speaking of that, I think I'm stuck," says the whale shark.

"Yeah, yeah, I know the drill," I tell her. "You're stuck between life and death. Tethered to this earthly coil. And only I can set you free and release you to the great ocean in the sky."

She shakes her enormous head. "No, bro. I just mean, I think my dorsal fin is stuck in your ceiling fan."

Ah. Classic.

"Lemme help you out with that, sister." Wally gives her a tug, freeing her from the grasp of my lighting fixture.

"Aw, yeah," the whale shark says, flopping onto my bed and soaking my bedclothes with her briny drippiness. "Hey, you know what I could go for right about now? Some plankton. Like, some primo choice plankton. You guys got any plankton like that around this place?"

"Sorry," I tell her. "All out of plankton. I have Fritos."

Wally pulls out the Monopoly board and starts setting up the pieces.

"All righty!" says Wally, rubbing his fins together. He turns to Drumstick with a ferocious grin. "Start dealing out that funny money, seagull. It's the two of us against you. You're goin' down, and this time, we're taking all of your cash!"

"What's cash?" asks the whale shark, leaning over the Monopoly board. "Can you eat it?"

Wally swats me on the shoulder. "You better get hopping, little man," he says. "At this rate, there's gonna be a whole school of us crammed in here."

The narwhal's not wrong. And the cramped quarters and seaside stench are wearing on my frayed nerves as it is. Questions must be answered. Before this happens again.

Darvish picked a terrible time to abandon me. I could use a little auditory processing right about now.

I turn to the whale shark. "How did this happen?" I ask her.

"There I was," she says. "Making some sweet waves just off Lighthouse Point."

"Hey! Me too!" cries Wally. "Innocent as can be, just helping myself to herring—"

"Me myself, I'm more of a plankton lady," says the whale shark. "Know what I'm sayin'?"

"And suddenly BOOM!" continues Wally. "Net over the head!"

"Me too!" cries the whale shark. "I didn't see any faces, but those humans with their nasty old nets and their weird people-hands..."

"Did you see the Iron Lady?" asks Wally.

"Oh my gosh!" the shark confirms. "Yes! I thrashed out at her, but she was very strong! *¡Muy sólido!*"

"That's my teacher!" I tell them. "And believe me, she's capable of worse than this. You should see the math homework she gives us."

This is just further confirmation of everything I suspected. And it's time to bring this corruption and villainy to an end, once and for all.

"Once and for all!" I announce with no shortage of flair. "We are going back into Bellingham Manor to find the proof. And we're not coming out without it!"

"Oh man," says Drumstick nervously. "That sounds scary. And dangerous."

This chicken worries way too much.

I, however, do not. Tonight, I will go to bed with the confidence of a man with a plan. With the self-assurance of a man who knows tomorrow will bring new hope.

With the wet pajamas of a man with soggy sheets.

35

Antarctica is the coldest place on Earth.

Temperatures on its frozen tundra can reach a crisp negative 133 degrees.

Besides penguins, very little life can survive in this barren wasteland of ice.

And yet, today, Antarctica has been demoted to second place. Because there is one place on earth chillier than our southernmost continent.

The desk behind Darvish.

Because that's where I'm sitting. And things are frosty between us.

I, however, am a survivor. An emperor penguin in the face of his glacial countenance. So I press on, valiant in my efforts to break the ice.

"Our teacher has struck again," I whisper. "Darvish, her depravity knows no bounds."

His eyes dart back at me. But he says nothing. Brrr.

"It happened at the same place, Darvish," I hiss. "Just off Lighthouse Point."

Nothing. Ice-pop city.

"They both got netted in Snarbly Bay," I hiss more loudly. "And they both saw the Iron Lady!"

"You're going to get us in trouble," says Darvish tersely.

"Darvish, we're already in trouble!" I hiss. "We're eating trouble three meals a day! We're up to our eyelids in the stuff! What can this woman do to us that she hasn't already done?"

"She could throw her desk at us, that's what," he hisses. "Or worse, give us detention."

But he turns around. "What kind of animal is it anyway?"

His curiosity has gotten the better of him. The ice is not broken. The permafrost has not fully thawed. But I have warmed the bitter exterior of his anger and drawn him out of his iceberg with my intrigue and mysterious nature. It's a start.

"It's an even bigger whale than last time," I tell him. "It's a whale shark."

He shakes his head. "A whale shark isn't a whale. It's a fish."

I acquiesce. I do not wish to upset him again. But

if you ask me, the world of aquatic animal naming is a screwy, topsy-turvy place. The narwhal is a whale, but the thing that has *whale* in its name...is a fish? Who decided this?

"Well, whatever she is, she's massive," I say. "And she's gluttonous. Especially for plankton. And Fritos."

"I wish I could see her," says Darvish in a hushed voice. "I've always wanted to see a whale shark. They're so majestic."

"I don't know if I'd call her majestic," I say. "But she's definitely dead. And Miss Mary is the vile culprit."

His eyes dart back up to the front of the classroom. Miss Mary prattles away about the American Revolution, oblivious to the fact that a revolution of another sort is being plotted in her midst.

"I can't believe she would do this," says Darvish.

"The facts don't lie," I tell him. "Fact number one: Both Wally and Tiny saw the Iron Lady right before they died!"

"Tiny?" he asks.

Yes. I've named the whale shark Tiny. What about it?

I continue my litany of logic. "Fact number two: Miss Mary is known as the Iron Lady. She has the wrestling belt to prove it."

His eyes dart to the credenza in question. "I guess that's true."

"Fact number three: The narwhal and the whale

shark both described her to a T. Strong. Built. *Muy sólido.* Which I'm pretty sure is Spanish for 'lover of math homework.' There can be no doubt."

Darvish looks wistfully at our teacher. "She seems so nice."

"The Iron Lady has taken you for a ride, Darvish," I tell my friend. "She is a felonious agent of the underworld. The dark, seedy underbelly of black-market animal poaching."

"Gosh. If that's true, this is big." He scratches his head nervously. "But we need hard proof."

"That's right," I tell him. "We need to get back into Bellingham Manor."

He nods his head. "Fine. We'll go tomorrow," he whispers. "After school. I'll talk to Dimitri."

That's what I like to hear. We are the kings of the arctic tundra. The penguin boys, together again.

"That's my boy!" I cry.

He bristles at this and turns around. "I'm not your boy," he mutters. "This changes nothing."

But his sudden movement has alerted the authorities to our presence. And by "authorities," I mean Miss Mary.

"Rex?" says Miss Mary coldly. "Darvish? What's going on back there?"

Nothing, that's what. Just two innocent penguins, plotting a revolution.

36

At the far end of the recess yard, there is a set of metal monkey bars.

It is old.

And rusty.

A relic from a bygone era.

That's where I see Tiny when I get out of school at three o'clock.

Hanging upside down.

Snatching butterflies out of the air.

And eating them.

"What are you doing here?" I ask her. I climb up the corroded bars to sit next to her.

"I was feeling all cooped up in that room," she says, dangling from the upper bar. "Yo, I'm a big fish. I need wide-open spaces. Endless reefs in which to roam, know what I'm sayin'?"

"Yeah," I say. "I've been sitting at a desk for the last six hours." If I'm honest, I'm feeling a little cooped up myself.

I loop my legs under the bars, and we hang there together. Upside down. In companionable silence.

For many years, I have dreamed of having a dog. An unconditional friend who pines for my presence while I am away. A faithful boon companion who waits loyally for me at the edge of the school grounds.

I never got a dog. I got a chicken. And a narwhal. And a whale shark.

None of those are dogs. And no amount of wishing will make them go bowwow.

And yet. Finding Tiny waiting for me after school . . . well, it warms the frostbitten cockles of my heart. It really does.

She snatches another butterfly from the air and pops it into her mouth.

Tomorrow, Darvish and I are meeting up with Dimitri Bellingham. We're going to Bellingham Manor. And we're going to find this narwhal head once and for all.

But in the meantime, it's kind of nice just quietly dangling from the monkey bars with a really big fish.

Tiny sighs.

"What's wrong?" I ask, pulling myself up.

"I miss Paco," she says.

"Isn't that the little squid you ate?" I clarify.

"Yeah," she says defensively. "Like, accidentally, okay?"

"Okay," I say.

"Just 'cause I gobbled him up doesn't mean he wasn't my best friend," she says sadly. "He was. That little squid was my best friend. There. I said it."

"Well, he's dead," I tell her.

"Yo! I know that already!" she says. "Way to ruin a tender moment!"

"No," I say, backpedaling. "I mean, he's dead. And you're dead. So once we figure this whole thing out and get you spiritually unstuck . . ." I trail off.

"What?" she asks, pulling herself upright.

"I don't know," I say wistfully. "Maybe you'll see him again. Maybe...he'll forgive you. Maybe...just maybe, you can patch things up again."

We sit there quietly, watching the butterflies flit through the air.

"That would be nice," Tiny finally says. "You don't really realize how much you need somebody until they're gone."

"Yeah," I say. "I know."

She gulps down another butterfly. "You know what else?" she asks.

"What?" I ask.

"These little bugs taste a lot like plankton," she says. "Except the red ones. Those taste like lobster."

I nod in understanding. I have had my fair share of run-ins with lobster. And heartbreak. I make a mental note to avoid the red ones.

37

I have grown a beard.

It is a Bandholz beard. Also known as a lumberjack.

It is luxurious. And woolly. And also fake.

"Why do you have a fake beard on?" asks Dimitri Bellingham.

"My reasons are my own," I tell him. Darvish just sighs.

In addition to being my own, my reasons should be self-evident to all. While scouring the Bellingham estate for clues, I could run into my nemesis. No, I'm not talking about Sami Mulpepper. I am not even talking about Charlotte Doyle. Though that girl is on my list.

I am talking, of course, about Mary-Kate Mary. Miss Mary thinks I have been growing my facial hair out. It would be suspicious for it not to have made some progress since I last saw her. And, owing to my macho build and virile demeanor, I believe this beard represents the realistic amount of new growth since this afternoon.

I have convinced Dimitri Bellingham to give us the grand tour of his rad pad. Aka show us around while I secretly scour the premises for proof of my teacher's shady dealings with the criminal underworld. Dimitri Bellingham is oblivious to our true purpose.

Darvish has agreed to accompany me on this mission, but as a business colleague, not as a friend. And I believe he still has his doubts about our teacher's involvement. He will require hard evidence to be fully convinced. So my eyes are peeled.

This place is a taxidermist's fairyland. Aka Holly Creskin's worst nightmare. Everywhere, there are heads. Wild boars from Borneo. Moose from the Arctic Circle. Zebra from Ethiopia.

But no narwhals from Lighthouse Point.

"No chickens, either," says Drumstick, staring around morosely. "That's a relief."

"Nobody's going to put a scrawny seagull like you on the wall, hot wings," says Wally. "You'd barely make a decent appetizer."

"Oh snap, you did not just say that!" cries the whale

shark. "You hear that, little seagull? Big Wally just called you hot wings!"

This place is a shrine to bad taste. And it doesn't just specialize in heads. Exotic hunting weapons also hang from every surface.

Elephant guns from Mozambique. Blowguns from Ecuador. Crossbows from New Jersey.

Further evidence that we are in the nest of a viper.

"All right," whispers Darvish, staring morosely at the heads. "This is yucky, but it's not proof of anything."

The kid's right. Dimitri Bellingham has shown us the kitchen, the ballroom, the library, the conservatory, the main hall, the dining room, and twelve bathrooms. But still no narwhal head. We'll never cover this whole place with him holding back like this.

"Lots of heads," I tell Dimitri Bellingham.

"Yeah, sorry, guys," he says sheepishly. "My mom is really into hunting."

"Nay, Dimitri Bellingham." I try to coax him out. "I find these heads to be a real statement. It is a testament to good and tasteful design!"

"No," he says. "It's just embarrassing. And gross. I keep telling her that dead animals aren't cool. But she just says I lack the killer instinct." He shrugs self-consciously. "My mom and I don't see eye to eye on a lot of things. It's kind of a problem. She says I'll never be able to inherit her empire with my softhearted attitudes."

"Well, it sure looks like she's been everywhere," says Darvish. "Any fish heads hung anywhere? Or aquatic mammals?"

Aw. My baby Darvish is all grown up and manipulating Dimitri Bellingham.

"No fish heads," says Dimitri. "There's a giant swordfish mounted in the billiard room. But—ooh! Speaking of fish, let me show you something really cool!"

He leads us down a grand set of stairs. We make a right. Then a left. Then another right. And we finally arrive in a massive chamber.

Before us is the biggest aquarium I've ever seen. Floor-to-ceiling glass, the length of the hallway.

"Wow," says Darvish in awe. "That's a big fish tank."

Dimitri Bellingham beams. "Three million gallons of water. I asked my mom if we could do a fish tank. I was thinking something normal size. But Mom believes that if you're going to do something, do it big."

"But no fish," Wally points out.

"And no plankton, neither," says Tiny. "Not cool. Not cool."

"No fish?" I ask.

"Not yet," Dimitri Bellingham answers. "Mom says she's going to fill it for me with all kinds of exotic species. But I'll believe it when I see it. Like most things involving me, she hasn't gotten around to it yet."

The aquarium is cool. Even cooler is what's in it. Old-timey shipwrecks litter the bottom. Like buried treasure.

"Mom had these shipwrecks salvaged and brought in from all over the world," says Dimitri Bellingham.

"Go big or go home," says Darvish. "Right?"

"Yep," says Dimitri. "That ship down there is called the *Hidden Mischief*. It sank off the Swedish coast in 1671." He points to another. "That one is the *Shikoku*, salvaged from the Sea of Japan."

The history of the world's failure at sea is long. And boring. My eyes dart around the long hall, searching desperately for the evidence we need. I can sense it. Our time here is running short. As is my attention span. And still, we're empty-handed.

Dimitri Bellingham points into the tank. "That figurehead was recovered from a ship called the *Maiden Voyage*. It's one of the very few metal figureheads made in the 1700s."

"That's her!" says Wally, pointing.

I turn back to the aquarium. "What?"

"Oh, I was just saying that not many figureheads were made out of metal," says Dimitri Bellingham.

But I've tuned this kid out.

"That's the Iron Lady!" Wally says again, grabbing my arm and pointing into the tank.

I scan the aquarium. There's no sign of Miss Mary. No Iron Lady.

"Yup," agrees Tiny. "That's her, all right."

All I see is a big metal statue. Well, part of a statue. The upper half of a giant woman, mounted to the aquarium wall. One of those thingies that goes on the front of a ship.

A figure eight.

Wally looks me in the eyes. "That's the last thing I saw before I croaked," he says. "That lady. That's the Iron Lady."

Realization hits me like a two-ton woman made of metal. The Iron Lady is not Miss Mary. It's a statue.

Which would mean Miss Mary isn't involved in this

at all. She obviously got that tattoo just to throw me off the scent! It's a devious move on her part.

Which means Wally and Tiny kicked the bucket in this aquarium. Which means that the real person behind all of this is...

Of course.

"Excuse me," says a voice from behind us. "Can I ask what you're all doing down here?"

I turn. And I see her.

Notorious hunter of fuzzy creatures everywhere. Slayer of furry beasts great and small. My Bandholz beard quivers in fear for its fuzzy, furry life.

Because standing before us... is Trinity Bellingham.

38

I saw an alien horror movie once.

It was about the misadventures of a space crew being chased by an acid-spitting alien. Seeing it was ill-advised. It left me with the cold sweats and haunted my sleep for weeks afterward.

Zero stars. Would not recommend.

I think it had the word *alien* in the title. I can't remember. Which is just as well. I don't need a libel lawsuit on my hands.

The point is this: At the end of the movie, the heroine opened the airlock door, sucking everything out of the room. Including the acid-spitting alien. Out into the cold vacuum of space.

I know this feeling too well.

Because at the sight of Trinity Bellingham, every bit of precious oxygen is sucked from the inside of my body. Out into the cold vacuum of the hallway. Also a little bit of spit.

"Little boy," says Trinity Bellingham, searching me like a cat eyeballing a canary. "Did you just spit on my thirty-thousand-dollar Persian rug?"

I don't have an answer. Except maybe don't pay that kind of cash for things that people might accidentally spit on. But I don't say that. Because I'm trying not to pee my pants. On her thirty-thousand-dollar Persian rug.

So I say the one thing that makes sense under these tense circumstances.

"Doi—eeeeeeeeeeee."

"Dimitri," she says stiffly. "If you're going to bring people onto my estate, I do wish you'd keep them in your playhouse. We didn't spend all that money for it to sit empty while some little boy drools on my carpeting or accidentally breaks my aquarium."

"Don't you mean *my* aquarium?" asks Dimitri.

"Pish-posh, son," she says. "Now, who are these ragamuffins?"

"Mom, this is Rex and Darvish," says Dimitri Bellingham. "They're my new friends."

"Ah," says Trinity Bellingham. "Well, your one friend looks like he could do with a shave. Perhaps take them to your playhouse, dear. Before he starts shedding."

"Fine," says Dimitri Bellingham.

"You know I don't really like people down here near the aquarium," Trinity Bellingham says. "It's not presentable yet."

"Come on, guys," says Dimitri Bellingham, leading us up the hall.

"Dimitri, be sure not to neglect Aldo and Sidharth," Trinity says. "They're your friends, too. And they don't shed. Or dribble on the rug."

Dimitri Bellingham sighs in frustration. "I don't need bodyguards, Mom. I told you."

"Vigilance, Dimitri!" she roars after us. "That is how the hunter gets the prize! Unceasing vigilance!"

"Yeah, Mom," he says, huffing past her. "But I'm not a hunter."

"No, boy," I hear her whisper. "No, you are not."

I feel her snake eyes follow us up the hallway. Right before we turn the corner, I risk a glance back.

She's gone.

Leaving me wondering: Was she ever there in the first place? Was she a figment of my fevered imagination? And why do I have the cold sweats?

I don't have any answers.

But I do know this: If those movie producers ever decide to do a sequel to that alien movie, I know who they could get to play the acid-spitting alien.

39

We have escaped the House of Horrors with our lives.

Barely.

I feel certain that, if Trinity Bellingham had known our true intentions, Darvish and I would just be two more heads on her wall of doom.

But the close call has left Darvish more unsettled than normal. He's gibbering nonsense like a mental patient.

"You were wrong," Darvish says.

See? Nonsense.

"Miss Mary had nothing to do with it," he points out. "And neither did the Russians."

Poor guy. I try my best to humor him. "My sweet

frittata," I say to him. "My queso omelet. Don't you see? Miss Mary and the Russians were just a false trail. A cleverly laid ruse devised by the real enemy. And you fell for it hook, line, and sinker."

"Why are you calling me those things?" he asks. "Frittata? Omelet?"

"Because you are an egg," I tell him softly. "Delicate. Easily cracked. Often filled with misguided notions and strange contents. Like mushrooms. Who puts mushrooms in an omelet? Honestly."

"Rex."

"I'm just trying to appease your tender constitution with light-hearted nicknames."

"I'm not an egg," he says. "But I'm glad to get out of that place. That lady is scary."

"That is because Trinity Bellingham is a villain," I tell him. "Wally and Tiny died in her aquarium. She's behind all of this."

"You were right about her," he says.

"Or course I was, Darvish. Good job." At last. He's talking sense again. But I do not belabor the point. I want him to feel good about his meager contributions to our predicament. Especially in his current condition.

"But what are we going to DO about it?" he cries, pacing nervously around my kitchen.

"Calm down, Darvish," I tell him. "You don't want to overexcite yourself again."

"How can I calm down?" he says, flailing his arms like a pair of gummy worms. "Finding that figurehead proves it was her."

"Figure eight," I say.

"But that's not enough!" he says.

"Keep it together, Darvish," I tell him calmly. "We have two eyewitnesses."

Darvish grabs me by the collar. "But our eyewitnesses ARE DEAD SEA CREATURES!" There is mania in his eyes. He's teetering on the brink.

But even in his addled state, he has a point. Wally's and Tiny's testimonies will hardly hold up in a court of law.

Darvish flounces away from me, knocking the stack of mail off the counter.

"Darvish. Buddy. Try to breathe," I tell him.

"I'm not your buddy," he reminds me.

"Fine" I say, bending down to retrieve the scattered envelopes from the floor. "But settle down anyway. You're like a bullwhip in a china shop."

"The saying is 'bull in a china shop,'" he points out. "Not bullwhip."

"Please don't correct me," I tell him. "You know it makes me crazy. At least one of us needs to keep it together."

But maybe I am going crazy. Because I'm holding the answer in my hand. There it is. Among the electric bill. And the grocery store circular. And the postcard advertising a new tanning place.

It's an invitation. To Mom's work thing. I completely forgot about it.

You are cordially invited to
THE BELLINGHAM GALA
for Wildlife Preservation
Saturday, April 3
8 p.m.
Bellingham Manor
Formal Attire Is Requested

"This is it!" I cry, waving the invitation in the air.

"What is?" asks Darvish, taking the invitation.

Victory is mine. My wheels are turning fast. I'm like a bulldozer in a china shop, and there's no stopping me now.

"I have to go to this gala thing," I say. "My mom works for that fiendish woman."

"Wildlife preservation?!" Darvish cries, reading the invitation. "Trinity Bellingham is one of the world's most famous hunters! What does she know about preserving wildlife?"

"Darvish!" I scold. "Please! Quit fixating on unrelated details! I will be deep behind enemy lines. It will be crowded. There will be food. Music. Distractions. The perfect opportunity for me to investigate further and find the solid proof we need!"

"I'm going with you," says Darvish, throwing the invitation to the ground decisively.

My brave little Southwest Skillet Scramble.

"If you think you're up to it," I say. "I cannot deny, it's a good idea. When scouting in hostile territory, a second person is always helpful to draw enemy fire when the shooting starts."

Of course, I would hate to lose Darvish right when I am on the verge of winning him back. He is a good egg. And he's come such a long way. But it's a risk I'm willing to take.

"Shooting?" he says. "You don't think there will really be any shooting, do you?"

"You're fixating again, Darvish," I point out. "Now, you'll have to rent a tuxedo."

He grimaces with distaste. "I'm not renting a tux," he says. "I'm uncomfortable wearing clothes that lots of other people have worn."

"Wake up, son!" I cry. "This is a classy affair of the upper crust! There could be movie stars. Foreign dignitaries! Jugglers! You can't show up in your khakis looking like common riffraff!"

"You don't have to worry about that," he says. "I own my own tuxedo."

Of course he does. Because that's what weirdos do. Own tuxedos.

40

With our foolproof plan in place, all we can do is wait.

Waiting is the worst. It can unravel the most tightly wound mind. Unsteady the steadiest nerves. Fray the spirit of the unfrayable.

I need respite. Distraction. A change of scenery.

Also, I can't stand the smell of my own room any longer.

I cannot go to Darvish's house. Things are still quite frosty between us. Plus, I think they're having lobster mac and cheese for dinner. So, ew.

Therefore, I have retreated to a picnic table in the park. To watch the Monopoly match of the century.

Wally has removed several hotels from his mouth and placed them on Park Place. And Boardwalk. Which he now owns. He also owns Reading Railroad. Pennsylvania Railroad. Water Works. New York Avenue. And numerous other high-profile properties.

His empire is vast. His side of the board is fat with cash. I believe my narwhal may finally have gotten his groove.

Drumstick owns Baltic Avenue. Which any Monopoly aficionado will tell you is a sad state of affairs.

Tiny was bankrupted long ago and is somewhere nearby chasing butterflies.

And it is at this tense moment, it is as these two juggernauts of industry go head-to-head, that disaster strikes.

Holly Creskin shows up. Ninny extraordinaire. Flying a Pegasus kite.

"Hi, Rex!" she chirps. "What are you doing?"

"Isn't it obvious, Holly Creskin?" I tell her. "I am watching the Monopoly match of the century."

"Ooh! Can I play?" she asks.

"No, Holly Creskin," I answer. "This game is weeks in the making. The money was dealt two hours ago. And only now am I on the cusp of witnessing long-awaited triumph."

"Oh." She shoots me an odd look. I am aware that,

to her, I look like a maniac sitting alone with a Monopoly board. But I cannot be bothered with what Holly Creskin thinks.

"Do you like my kite?" she asks.

I spare a glance. "It's adequate, as far as kites go."

"It's a Pegasus."

"I know what a Pegasus is, Holly Creskin," I say. "I sit through the same boring biology lessons that you do."

"Okay," she says, tugging her kite string. "Well, bye. Have fun playing with yourself."

"I do not play with myself, Holly Creskin!" I call after her. "I am bearing witness to a match of historic proportions!"

But she is gone. Taking her anatomically incorrect kite with her.

Drumstick rolls his dice and moves his piece, landing squarely on New York Avenue.

"That's two houses and two hotels!" roars Wally. "Pay up, seagull!"

My chicken is left with one hundred dollars to his name. One hundred measly clams stand between this bird and total annihilation. Sweet narwhal victory is at hand!

And it is at this critical moment that the unthinkable happens.

Holly Creskin, running blindly across the park

with her kite in tow, trips on my butterfly-chasing whale shark.

(Don't ask me how these ghosts are forever grabbing stuff and bumping into things. I once had a dead rhino that couldn't keep her mitts off my lunch. It was a whole thing.)

The point is, Holly Creskin goes flying into a bush.

And her kite string goes slack.

And her Pegasus goes on a free-falling reign of terror...right onto our Monopoly board.

Houses clatter. Hotels crumble. Cash scatters to the four winds.

Wally withdraws the skewered Monopoly board from atop his horn. He looks down at the remains of his vast and expansive empire. And he shrugs at the chicken.

"We're gonna call that a win for me," he says.

"Yeah," says Drumstick. "Okay."

The game of the century. Brought to heel by the kite of a ninny.

Classic.

41

It is Saturday. April 3. G-Day.

G stands for Gala. And Glorious victory. And Gee, I look Good in this tux.

Because two things are clear.

One: I am a vision.

And two: Trinity Bellingham is a master of manipulation. The woman is giving a great speech. And the genteel bootlickers who have gathered at this little soiree are lapping it up.

"You know," she says to the well-heeled crowd, "a lot of people think hunters don't care about wildlife. Nothing could be further from the truth. Hunters like me donate and raise more funds for wildlife conservation than any other group. Your contributions tonight will help save hundreds of species around the world. So thank you! Because one of these days, my wall is going to have a Nile crocodile on it. And it's because you helped keep a healthy population of them on the planet!"

The crowd laughs at her joke. But I see through the light-hearted facade to the dark nature within.

Trinity Bellingham is duplicitous. Fake. Wily and cunning, like a predatory cobra, hypnotizing her prey before she swallows it whole.

Also, she serves excellent crab puffs at these things.

I look across the room to check the positions of Wally, Tiny, and Drumstick. Darvish and I have stationed them on the perimeter of the room to serve as lookouts. Also, because they make a soggy mess everywhere they go.

I even thought about roping Dimitri Bellingham into doing some light scouting for our cause, but he's nowhere to be seen. Maybe Mommy doesn't allow him to attend these fancy shindigs.

Wally shoots me a thumbs-up, and I turn to consult with Darvish.

That's when I catch sight of something completely unexpected. Something that causes me a momentary flashback of pain and regret. Something that triggers memories from my recent past, from which I may never fully recover.

And that something is Sami Mulpepper in a ball

gown. The same one she wore to the Evening of Enchantment Dance. Blue-green with little flowers.

"Sami!" Darvish says. "What are you doing here?"

"Hey, guys," says Sami Mulpepper. "My dad is the state police commissioner. So he always gets invited to these fancy-pants parties. Why are you here?"

"For no reason whatsoever!" I say smoothly.

"Rex's mom works for Trinity Bellingham," says Darvish, overexplaining as usual.

"Ah!" Sami Mulpepper nods. "Well, looking sharp, fellas!"

I have no response to this. Thankfully, something catches my eye. It's Tiny. From her vantage point across the room, she is waving her huge fins and pointing into the crowd.

At Trinity Bellingham. The woman is a picture of social grace. Gripping hands and waving at the well-dressed men and women of Middling Falls society. Sashaying her way through the crowd. Sashaying directly toward us.

"Abort!" I hiss to Darvish. "Abandon ship! Swallow your cyanide pill! She's onto us!"

"Rebecca!" croons Trinity Bellingham, hugging my mother. "I'm so glad you could be here! And you brought your family! How wonderful."

My mother is dressed in a fancy cocktail dress. She is wearing pearls. And she apparently goes by "Rebecca" now. The world has gone topsy-turvy.

"Thanks for having us, Trinity," gushes my mom. "I'd like you to meet my husband, Jake, my son, Rex, and his friend Darvish."

"Ah, you're Dimitri's little friends!" says Trinity Bellingham, a big smile plastered across her face. It is a smile that hides the beast that lives within. But she's not fooling anybody.

Actually, she is fooling everybody. But not me and Darvish. We've got her number.

"Welcome to you all!" she says. "Now, if you'll excuse me. I need to go check in with the caterers. It seems they've run out of crab puffs. Can you imagine?"

I turn to Darvish. "Now's our chance."

"To do what?" he asks.

"To slip away," I tell him. "Find the security room. Track down the footage that seals Trinity Bellingham's fate. And end her reign of carnage."

He grabs something from my hors d'oeuvre plate and pops it into his mouth. "Let's go."

We sneak away from my hobnobbing parents. We skulk back from the gilded crowds. We slink down a back hallway, Wally, Tiny, and Drumstick trailing in our wake. I focus my mind on the covert task ahead. But one thought haunts me.

A thought so terrible that it makes my head spin and my stomach turn.

I'm pretty sure Darvish just ate the last crab puff.

42

We have taken approximately four million steps. I haven't been counting. But I'm sure it is a close approximation.

And we are no closer to finding the truth than when we started. But I could be wrong. Maybe the proof we seek is just around the next bend. I don't know.

That is because we are rats in a maze. It is a maze made of deception. And intrigue. But also of walls. And endless hallways. And limitless locked doors. And tireless corridors. That stretch on and on. With no end.

In other words, this mansion is really big. And we are lost.

"We live here now, Darvish," I tell my friend. "And we shall die here."

It's clear we will perish of thirst before we find our way back to the civilized world of ball gowns and crab puffs. But just when I think all hope is lost, Darvish tries another door.

And this one opens.

"At last," I cry. "The security room. Herein lies the video footage that will send Trinity Bellingham to the big house for all time."

"Why would the one door that's unlocked be the security room?" asks Darvish.

He knows it drives me mental when he contradicts me. Yet he persists.

But it is not the security room. Before us lies a pool the size of a football field. A pool that holds numerous shipwrecks. And a metal figure eight of a lady. And three million gallons of water. Which, when you compare it to the number of steps we've taken tonight, is nothing.

We have found the aquarium. Or the *top* of the aquarium. A network of pipes and tanks zigzags overhead. At the far end, huge doors lead outside. To a dock. And the ocean.

And they're open.

"This is the place," says Wally, shaking his long horn in consternation. "I can still remember the smell."

"Mm-hm. This is the place, all right," agrees Tiny. She shuffles toward the enormous bay doors. "They brought me in through there. Slid me down that ramp. And dropped me into the water."

"Rex. Check this out," says Darvish. He's kneeling beside the pool, shaking a little vial.

"Darvish. Please," I say. "This is a crime scene. Don't contaminate the evidence with your crab-puffy hands and your devil-may-care attitude."

Darvish rolls his eyes. "I'm not contaminating anything."

"Then what are you doing?" I ask.

"I'm checking the water," says Darvish. "The pH levels are way out of whack, Rex."

I raise an eyebrow at him. "And you always carry your dad's pH kit around with you?"

He shrugs self-consciously. "I told you. It relaxes me."

"Well, that's great work!" I tell him. "Fantastic. Amazing. Except for one thing. I have no idea what pH is."

He clears his throat like a little tuxedo-wearing professor about to give a lecture. "pH measures the concentration of hydrogen ions in the water. It checks for acidity and—"

"Okay, okay," I jump in. I immediately regret opening the door into the magical world of pH. I hold up my hand. "Sorry," I say. "It's fascinating stuff, Darvish. Truly. But for the sake of time, jump to the end."

"It's complicated," he says with a sigh. "What matters is that the pH tells me that no marine life could stay alive in this water. Rex . . . *this* is the bad water."

"Bad water," whispers Drumstick.

"Bad water," whispers Wally.

"Bad water," whispers Tiny. A shiver ripples through them all.

"Bad water?" says a female voice. "Just what exactly do you gentlemen think you're doing?"

That's when we turn. And see her.

We are so busted.

43

Sami Mulpepper. Auburn-haired straight-A student. Soup-scented reader of *Charlotte Doyle*. Girl incapable of making brownies.

She has followed us.

Classic.

"What's going on here, guys?" asks Sami Mulpepper suspiciously. "I don't think you're supposed to be in here."

"Sami!" cries Darvish.

"You guys!" calls Sami Mulpepper.

"Rex!" cries Darvish.

"The last thing we need is more witnesses," says Wally. He nods at Sami Mulpepper and punches his fin into the other. "You want I should take care of her?"

"Yeesh." Drumstick grimaces. "Taken out by a narwhal horn. Not a nice way to go."

"You know what I could do?" says Tiny. "I could just gobble her up, mkay? I could probably do it in one gulp. She'd barely feel a thing."

I hold up my hands. "EVERYBODY JUST BE QUIET!" I yell.

My voice echoes off the pipes and fades into silence.

I need a moment to myself. A moment to think. A moment to contemplate the situation.

I walk the length of the pool. Up the slick ramp. Through the giant open doors. Onto the dock outside. And into the night air.

I peer over the lapping ocean water. Into the darkness.

And I see a light. The light of a boat.

"Darvish," I say softly. "Come here."

In moments, I am surrounded by my entourage. Not just Darvish. But a full and actual entourage.

"She's not checking on the caterers at all," I tell them. "That was just a ruse. She's using the gala as her alibi. Everyone will say she was there. Meanwhile, there she is." I point to the rocking light of the boat out on the bay. "She's doing it again."

"She who?" asks Sami Mulpepper.

"She Trinity Bellingham," I answer.

"What are we waiting for?" says Darvish. "We have to stop her!"

"You guys, is everything okay?" asks Sami Mulpepper nervously. "I'm going to go get my dad."

Darvish grabs my arm. "Maybe that's not a bad idea, Rex. Her dad is with the police."

"No," I tell him firmly. "No grown-ups."

"Why not?" he asks.

I grasp his face between my hands to focus his scattered attention. "*Think*, Darvish. Her dad is not going to believe us. And before you know it, my parents will be down here. And eventually, details about my connection with our finned friends are going to come out. Your permanent record will forever be tainted with the stain of this incident. And I'll be having biweekly appointments with the school counselor. And I don't have time for that!"

"My permanent record?" Darvish nods. "You're right. Sami! No grown-ups!"

I turn. "Sami Mulpepper, listen to me carefully. What I'm about to say is going to come as a shock. But you're going to have to trust me."

Darvish steps up. "You have to believe him. It's all true."

I take a deep breath. But I keep going. Before the courage fails me.

"I actually really liked it when you hugged me at the dance . . ."

Darvish smacks me on the shoulder. "Not that!"

The heart wants what the heart wants, Darvish. But he's right. There's a time and place. This probably isn't either.

I turn back to Sami Mulpepper. "Trinity Bellingham is out in that boat. Probably with a couple of her random thugs. She has already killed two giant fish—"

"Actually one fish and one aquatic mammal," chimes in Darvish. "A whale shark and a narwhal."

"Exactly!" I say. "And she's going to do it again right now, if we don't stop her."

Sami Mulpepper eyeballs us both skeptically. "How do you know this?" she asks.

"I can't tell you," I say.

"You wouldn't believe us if we did," says Darvish. "I barely believe it myself, and I'm living it."

"You just have to trust us," I say, peering into her blue-green eyes that shimmer with the reflection of her ball gown.

There is a long silence. The only sound I hear is the drip-drip-dripping of water from Tiny. The squich-squich-squiching of Wally shifting his weight nervously. And the munch-munch-munching of Drumstick chewing on a cocktail weenie.

Finally, Sami Mulpepper looks deep into my eyes. She sets her jaw. And she says the words that make my heart soar. "What are we waiting for? We've got to stop her."

Darvish and I release a sigh of relief.

"But how?" asks Darvish.

Sami Mulpepper points. "We'll take that speedboat."

She's right. There is a small speedboat moored to the end of the dock. It's a great idea. Except for one small flyswatter in the ointment.

"I don't know how to drive a speedboat," I admit.

"Me neither," says Darvish.

"I do," says Sami Mulpepper with a grin. "My dad taught me!"

She grabs a set of keys from a little hook near the boathouse. She dashes down the dock. And she leaps into the boat.

She looks back. "You guys coming?"

We pile in behind her and Sami Mulpepper turns the key in the ignition. The engine growls to life. The wind grabs her auburn tresses and whips them in the briny air. Yanking down a lever, she revs the motor, sending us, my dead pets, and the boat zipping away from the dock and into the murky waters of Snarbly Bay.

44

One thing is absolutely clear. I'm 80 percent sure I'm in love with Sami Mulpepper.

45

We are heroes, zooming through the mist of the night in a borrowed speedboat.

Toward victory. Toward glory. Toward a dolphin.

Because that is what we see as our boat approaches. Trinity Bellingham has netted herself another aquatic animal. Her random thugs are hauling it out of the water.

"Random thugs!" I cry. "Drop the porpoise!"

"That's a bottlenose dolphin," says Sami Mulpepper.

"Do not trouble me with superfluous details, Sami Mulpepper," I tell her. "We have caught them with their hands in the porpoise jar."

"Bottlenose-dolphin jar," says Darvish.

The thugs turn and face our approaching vessel.

Their hands release the controls. But their hands are far from empty. Because I see the glint of moonlight on metal. And then I realize what I'm seeing. The one thing that nobody, and I mean nobody, could have foreseen.

These thugs have guns.

"Oh my gosh," cries Darvish. "We're all going to die!"

"WE'RE ALL GOING TO DIE!" cries Drumstick, running in circles.

All this screeching is putting my frazzled nerves on end. "Wally, make that chicken be quiet," I cry. But Wally and Tiny are nowhere to be found. Typical. Happy to soak your sheets and wrinkle your Monopoly money, but when things get real, they run for cover like it's Fish Fry Friday.

"It doesn't matter if this goes on my permanent record," Darvish whimpers. He has curled himself into a fetal position on the floor of the boat. "Wanna know why? Wanna know? Because I'll be DEAD! That's why!"

"Don't fall into hysterics, Darvish," I tell him.

"They have guns!" he cries.

That may well be. But we are not without weapons of our own. For our boat holds the greatest weapon in Middling Falls. Possibly the entire Tri-County area.

My towering intellect. Also, Sami Mulpepper has placed a bowie knife into my hand.

"Take this," she says.

"Where did you get this?" I cry.

"It was in the boat," she answers. "Take it and hold on to something. I'm taking this baby up to ramming speed. At the moment I smash into them, you leap through the air and cut the dolphin free. We don't want it to drown when their boat sinks."

Who is this woman?! And where has she been all my life?

"Ramming speed?" cries Darvish in anguish. "Have you lost your mind?"

One of the thugs beckons to us. "All right, little girl. You bring that boat over here nice and slow. Nobody gets hurt."

"Little girl?" She grips the lever with white knuckles. "Hold on, guys."

Out of nowhere, BANG! A massive jolt hits the other boat.

It rocks. It rolls. It teeters. It totters. The thugs stagger. They reach out to steady themselves. And just like that...

PLOP! PLOOP! There go their guns. Right into the drink.

I alone see the seven-foot horn emerge from the water. "You just give the signal, boss," says Wally. "Any more rough stuff from these guys and they'll be sleepin' with the fishies. Ain't that right, sister?"

"Yo, you better believe it," says Tiny. "They're messing with Grande Bonita now!"

Suddenly, a voice from the other boat shatters the night air. "What is going on up here?" it cries. "Can't I trust you dum-dums to load this dolphin without sinking the whole boat?"

At last she emerges. Trinity Bellingham.

Clever woman. She has taken a leaf out of my book. She has disguised herself for her little nighttime dolphin-poaching trip. Not with anything quite as dashing as my Bandholz beard.

No. She has taken the guise of a young boy.

Slick blond hair. Argyle sweater. Two goons. The disguise is good. Thankfully, my agile mind is not easily tricked. But as her eyes turn to meet mine, I have to admit.

She looks exactly like Dimitri Bellingham.

46

Trinity Bellingham stands before me in a feeble disguise. But I see through her weak deception. And I tell her so with aplomb.

"I see through your weak deception, villain!" I yell. "But none of us are fooled! Reveal your true nature!"

"Hey, Rex. Hey Darvish," the boy says, voice cracking. "What are you guys doing out here?"

Something tells me Trinity Bellingham does not stand before me in a feeble disguise.

"Hey, Rex," says the real and actual Dimitri Bellingham. "What happened to your cool beard?"

The audacity! The gall! The sheer temerity! How dare this turncoat take the name of my Bandholz in vain. I'm half tempted to sic a fish on him. But no.

Violence is the weapon of a weak mind. And my mind is not weak.

Just stupid. Because I never suspected him. Perhaps my recent breakup with Darvish has clouded my good judgment. Thrown me off the scent. Caused my mental dexterity to slip in the mud.

Also, I've been thinking a lot about Sami Mulpepper lately.

Don't fall in love, people. It will ruin you.

"Dimitri?" says Darvish. "What are you doing?"

One of the goons whispers something in Dimitri Bellingham's ear. "No, I don't want you to silence them!" the kid shouts. "These are my friends! Go down belowdecks and wait there."

The goons retreat down a set of stairs. But I see what he's up to.

Dimitri Bellingham is going to attack. Like a mad dog. Like a cornered jackal. Like a desperate hyena. And he doesn't want any witnesses.

But Dimitri Bellingham doesn't know one important detail. I am an expert on canine behavior. And the one thing a cornered mongrel requires is a display of dominance to put him at ease.

I climb onto the hood of the boat and wave my arms until I am roughly double my size.

"UNHAND THAT BOTTLEROCKET DOLPHIN AND COME QUIETLY, DIMITRI BELLINGHAM!" I bark.

"I know this probably looks bad," he says.

"You guys know Dimitri Bellingham?" asks Sami Mulpepper, pulling the boat closer.

"It is a new and short-lived acquaintance," I tell her. "For, it turns out, the man is a rogue."

"Oh, don't say that," pleads Dimitri Bellingham.

"Dimitri, we know about the narwhal," says Darvish. "And the whale shark."

Dimitri Bellingham's face pales. "How do you know about that?"

"WE HAVE EYEWITNESSES!" I howl.

"My dad is the police commissioner," says Sami Mulpepper, following my lead. "When he finds out about this, you're going away!"

"Oh, good gosh," cries Dimitri Bellingham. "Guys, please don't say that. I'm not breaking any laws! I promise!" He reaches into the folds of his jacket.

"HANDS!" I roar. "HANDS WHERE I CAN SEE THEM! I HAVE A NARWHAL AND I'M NOT AFRAID TO USE IT!"

"I don't know what that means," says Dimitri Bellingham. "I'm just getting my permits out."

"Your what, now?" I ask.

"My mom has noncommercial hunting, fishing, and capture permits for just about every place in the world," he says, waving a sheaf of papers. "Including this bay! They cover our whole family! I haven't broken any laws!"

He hands the papers over to Darvish.

"Well, Darvish?" I ask. "Are they legitimate?"

"Dude, how do I know?" says Darvish. "I'm a sixth grader."

"Give me those," I say, snatching the papers away from his inexperienced hands. I scan the documents. "These are clearly papers," I announce. "And they have signatures. Which, to my practiced eye, makes them completely authentic."

"It doesn't matter if it's legal or not!" cries Darvish, rounding on Dimitri Bellingham. "It's messed up."

"I know," says Dimitri, his jaw quivering.

"Two animals died!" says Darvish.

"I know!" Dimitri repeats, wringing his hands. "I...I...I...I know." His eyes are filled with remorse

190

and dread. Also, tears. He gasps for air like a beached pufferfish.

"It's your pH," says Darvish, softening a bit. "It's all screwed up."

"My what?" asks Dimitri Bellingham, trying to focus.

"Your pH," Darvish repeats. "Dude, you can't just dump ocean animals in a pool. There's chemistry involved. You have to know what you're doing."

"I didn't think of that," he says. Tears stream down his face. He runs over to a panel of levers and throws a switch.

There's a grinding sound. The net holding the dolphin slowly lowers back into the water. The dolphin chirps happily, dives under the waves, and disappears.

"You're welcome, little buddy!" Wally calls after the retreating dolphin. "Stay outta trouble!"

Dimitri Bellingham's tears are turning to heaving sobs. "I didn't mean to hurt anything!" he cries. "You've got to believe me! I love animals!"

"A LIKELY STORY!" I shout from my authoritative perch.

"It's true!" he blubbers. "I don't even eat meat! I hate that my mom hunts animals. The last thing in the world I wanted to do was hurt one. Or kill one."

Sami Mulpepper crosses her arms. "Then why did you do it?"

"I just . . . wanted to show my mom."

He pauses. Sniffles. "She thinks I'm such a nothing," he says bitterly. *"It's a cutthroat world, Dimitri! You
must be ruthless! How will you ever inherit my empire if
you show no mettle?!"*

The tears stream silently down his cheeks. "That's
all I ever hear from her. She's been promising to finish the aquarium forever. But she's always too busy
running her business. Or off on another hunt halfway
around the world. I just wanted to show her . . ."

"What?" asks Darvish.

Dimitri wipes his nose with his sleeve. "That I
could do something special, too. My way. Without
being ruthless."

And that's when it happens. The one thing that
nobody, and I mean nobody, could have anticipated. I
feel a tear run down my face.

Dimitri looks up at us pleadingly. "Please don't tell
anybody," he begs. "I swear I'll never do anything like
this again. If she finds out, my mom will ship me off
to military school. *We've got to toughen you up! Put a
backbone into that spineless frame of yours!* She'll ship
me out. And that will be that."

There is silence. Just the sound of the waves lapping against the boats. And Drumstick loudly blowing
his beak.

"Well," says Sami Mulpepper. "He didn't technically break any laws."

"Two animals died, though," cries Darvish.

"Exactly," I say. "So it isn't really up to us."

I turn to Wally. And Tiny. Their heads bob above the water. It's hard to tell, since they're always moist. But I think there are tears in their eyes.

"I'm not here to ruin anybody's life," says Wally.

Tiny nods her enormous head. "Yeah, me neither," she says. "Know what? I think the whole reason I was kept from moving on was so I could stop it from happening to anybody else."

"Yeah," agrees Wally. "But I gotta admit. I'm not feeling so constipated anymore. Tethered neither."

I nod to Darvish. To Sami Mulpepper. And finally, to Dimitri Bellingham.

"Then it'll be our little secret," I say.

Sami Mulpepper spits in her hand and holds it out. Darvish follows suit. Then Dimitri. Then me. Drumstick throws his wing up there, just for good measure.

"I can't believe it," says Dimitri. "I've never had any friends. And the first time I have some, I get you." Dimitri Bellingham shakes his head in disbelief. "You guys are the best friends a guy could ever have."

I shrug. "Yeah, we are pretty great," I say.

"It's true," says Sami Mulpepper.

"The best," agrees Darvish.

Wally chimes in. "The kid ain't wrong, sport," he tells me with a wink.

"You got that right," says Tiny. "You're a true-blue pal, shorty. A friend to man and beast, living and dead alike!"

"Yep." I shoot a grin at my dead pets. "What can I say? It's a curse."

47

There are no more crab puffs at the gala. Possibly the entire Tri-County area. Maybe the world. Thanks to Darvish.

But there are mini pot stickers. For now. Drumstick is working diligently to add those to the endangered appetizers list as well.

And there is music. And champagne. And dancing. It is the kind of celebratory atmosphere one would expect on the heels of my stunning victory.

Wally and Tiny make their way through the crowd. They're leaving brackish puddles of seawater behind, and they don't care who knows it.

"You," says Wally, pointing at me.

"What?" I ask.

Wally snatches a couple glasses of champagne from a passing waiter's tray. He hands one to Tiny and holds his glass aloft.

"Here's to you, kiddo," says Wally. "I feel all spiritually footloose and fancy-free, thanks to you."

"Aw, yeah," says Tiny. "To the Rex-man!" She pours the contents down her gullet.

"You know, pal o' mine," says Wally, "in my neighborhood, we're not big with emotional displays. That touchy-feely stuff is not exactly up my alley, if you catch my drift. But what can I say?"

He grabs me around the neck and noogies me with his free fin. "You did good."

Tiny grins. "Well, I'm not afraid of a big squishy hug." She reaches down and squeezes me. "Yo, Rex. Thanks, baby," she says. "You're the best. *Buena onda.*"

Wally turns to Tiny and tips his miniature Monopoly top hat. "Whaddya say, sister? Would you honor me with one last dance?"

"Aw, yeah!" she says, holding out her fins. "Let's do this." She turns and shoots us a wink. "Later, fishes."

And with that, they waltz across the ballroom with a grace and elegance that belie their monstrous size and complete lack of legs. It is diminished only slightly by the trail of fat-cat aristocrats sliding tush over teakettle in the wake of their wet, slimy trail.

Drumstick screams, "KAMIKAZE!" and takes a sliding belly leap through the soaked dance floor.

And with a spin and a dip, the narwhal and the whale shark turn to mist. And fade away. Leaving nothing behind except a teeny Monopoly hat. And a puddle the size of Nebraska.

"They're gone," I tell Darvish, pulling a strand of seaweed from my hair. "I have untethered the tethered. Unplugged the spiritually constipated. I have un-netted these creatures from their earthbound purgatory."

"You didn't exactly do it all by yourself," Darvish points out.

"No," I concede. "You're right. Sami Mulpepper was a whiz with that speedboat."

"Okay," says Darvish, shaking his head. "Well, I'm honestly glad that's over."

There is an awkward pause. A chilly pause. Like, iceberg chilly.

Of course, it's possible that Trinity Bellingham's climate controls are just on the fritz. Yes, it's probably that. These enormous mansions are a nightmare to heat.

"Well," Darvish says stiffly, heading into the crowd. "I'm going to go mingle. I'll see you later."

"Darvish," I call.

But he doesn't look back. "Dude. I'll see you later."

And I watch him go. Off in search of the one thing that is as elusive in this hurly-burly world as a narwhal in a top hat. The one thing that will fill that aching hole inside of him. The one thing that we both know he'll never find.

More crab puffs.

"Rex!" Sami Mulpepper pushes her way through the mob, a big grin splitting her face. "That was so cool! How did you know about what Dimitri was doing? How long have you and Darvish been working on this?"

I have no answer for this.

She punches me roughly on the arm. "Are you going to fill me in?" she asks.

I shrug. "I haven't decided. Maybe someday."

She shakes her head with a smile. "All right, mystery man. Keep your little secrets."

I will. For tonight. Tomorrow? Well, anything could happen.

"So, now what?" Drumstick asks, dripping wet, his mouth full of cocktail meatballs.

Now what, indeed. This night has brought many things. I have faced gun-toting ruffians and lived to tell the tale. I have shown a wayward Dimitri Bellingham the error of his ways. I have sent Wally and Tiny on to the great Snarbly Bay in the sky.

However, one final injustice remains to be rectified.

"Sami Mulpepper," I say. "I sense that the orchestra has slowed their tempo. Which I think indicates a slow dance. Something we failed to do at the Evening of Enchantment."

I hold out my hand. And meet her eyes. "Would you care to dance?"

Her eyes widen slightly. "Just as friends?" she asks with a grin.

"Sure," I reply. I take her hand and lead her out onto the dance floor. "Let's start there."

48

I must say something to Darvish.

Something secretive. Something confidential. Something that, if questioned later by the nattering mass media, I will deny ever having said.

So I select a quiet location where we can discuss such issues uninterrupted.

The dumpster behind the school.

"This better be good, Rex," says Darvish. "I think I just put my shoe in mashed potatoes."

"I know how particular you are about your wardrobe, Darvish," I tell him. "And I know you are unhappy with me. So I will do you the service of getting right to the point."

I take a deep breath.

"I owe you an apology," I whisper.

"Wait, what?" he asks, unbelieving. "You owe me an apology?"

I nod. "Yes. I underestimated you."

"You underestimated me?" he asks.

Sweet Darvish. He has regressed into meaningless parroting. I blame myself. Yet, the words must be said.

"You showed real hutzpah on that boat," I tell him. "Gumption. Spirit."

"Wow," says a stunned Darvish. "Thanks."

"And that pH trick was great," I tell him with a pat on the shoulder. "You're coming along nicely."

"I am, huh?" he says with the ghost of a smile. "So that's all, then? I was useful to you?"

"You *were* useful," I say. "But...that's not all. Beyond that..."

"Beyond that?" he prompts.

I take a deep breath. This is harder than I anticipated. But I rally and press on.

"Beyond that," I say, "I would miss you if I accidentally ate you. You are my Paco."

"You lost me," he says.

"I'm being as clear as I can, buddy," I explain. "You are a little squid. You are *my* little squid."

"I don't know what that means," he says.

I pause. I scratch my head patiently.

"It means you are my best friend," I say quietly. "I need your help. No. I need *you*."

He stares at me in silence for a moment. "I have a life, too, you know," he says. "I have feelings and interests and all that other stuff."

"I know," I say sheepishly. "I will attempt to remember that."

"What about M&M?" he finally asks. "Are you sorry that you got me kicked out of M&M?"

I sigh. "I stand by my conviction that I did you a huge favor. Those M&M layabouts were dragging you down." I pause, mustering my newfound sensitive side. "But I understand that this game is important to you. I'm sorry I got you kicked out."

"You have to apologize to Iggy," says Darvish. "That's the only way he'll let me play again. And you have to join."

I take another deep breath. My nostrils fill with the smell of sour milk. And redemption.

"Fine," I say, feeling my spirit shrivel. "I will make an overture to Iggy Graminski. And I will give your new game a chance."

"Okay, then." He grins and claps me on the back. "Okay! Wowee."

"Wowee what?" I ask.

"An apology from Rex Dexter?" He lets out a little laugh. "I'd say we're both coming along nicely."

The light of truth streams down upon me. The warmth of goodness shines upon my heart. The torch of benevolence illuminates my soul. And I know I've done the right thing.

Only, it's not the light of truth. It's not the warmth of goodness. It's not the torch of benevolence.

It's blinding daylight filtering into my private domain. Somebody has opened the dumpster lid. And there's only one way a wolf deals with an invasion of his lair. A show of dominance.

"WHO DARES INVADE MY SANCTUM OF SOLITUDE?!" I roar.

I hear a weary sigh.

"Guys. This has got to stop," groans Ms. Kincaid.

49

ggy Graminski's candygram arrives the next day. It is sent through untraceable means. The card is composed of cutout magazine letters and reads as follows:

TO: IGGY GRAMINSKI,

ROSES ARE RED. ROGUES ARE SNEAKY. DARVISH IS SORRY FOR BEING SO CHEEKY.

AND SO ARE ANONYMOUS SOURCES NEAR HIM WHO SHALL REMAIN NAMELESS.

50

Never ask a dead chicken to work on your literature project for you. Because, rest assured, the results will be disappointing.

Drumstick was supposed to read *The True Confessions of Charlotte Doyle* for me. He didn't.

He was supposed to write a three-page book review of it for me. He failed to do so.

Instead, he watched the movie *Treasure Planet*. And then drew a little cartoon about it.

I don't know what this bird is playing at. But I am not pleased.

"Well, give me what you've done," I tell him. "My group is supposed to meet this afternoon. Maybe I can comb through your pathetic chicken scratching and salvage something to contribute."

"I don't have it," he cries, shrugging his wings.

"What do you mean, you don't have it?" I ask.

"I gave it to Sami," he says.

"Sami Mulpepper?" I ask. "How?"

"I stuck it in her purse at the Bellingham Gala," he says. "While you two were dancing."

This bird may well have crippled my entire academic career in one fell swoop.

"Why did you do that?" I ask.

"I assumed she's the leader of your group," he says.

"Why would you think that?" I cry, waving my arms frantically. "I bring the brownies! That has leadership written all over it!"

I dial Darvish's number. "Darvish. The chicken has doomed us all. When you finally graduate high school and find yourself at a rinky-dink state college with no prospects and no hope, you can thank my bird."

"Dude, what are you talking about?" he says. "Oh, by the way. Sami says we don't need to meet today to work on the literature project."

"Why not?" I ask.

"She says she got the cartoon you left in her purse. And I already gave her my work."

"That is not my cartoon!" I protest. "That is the work of a lazy and misguided barnyard fowl."

"Well, either way," Darvish says into the phone. "She says she knows we've been busy with this whole dolphin thing."

"Porpoise thing, Darvish."

"So she said she'd take care of it," he says.

"What does that mean?" I ask suspiciously.

"It means she's going to take all the stuff we each contributed and pull it together into a great report. She said to tell you not to sweat it. This time. Your brownies could be your contribution."

"Wait," I say. "So we're not meeting?"

"No," says Darvish. "But relax. With Sami taking charge of things, I'm pretty sure we'll get an A."

"I'm not worried about that," I tell him. "But I already had my dad make brownies for our meeting today."

"Wait," the chicken says. "Those brownies in the kitchen were for your group?"

"Yes," I tell him.

"Oops."

I hang up the phone.

First the chicken botches my literature project. Then he eats all my brownies.

This is some world-class guff, let me tell you.

51

I am under siege by bung-bears.

And I face the threat like any cutthroat rogue in similar circumstances would. By not hiding on my GM's lap.

Much to Darvish's delight, our Monsters & Mayhem rights have been reinstated. On a probationary basis.

I still fail to see the purpose of this game. There is no board. There are no pieces. There are no dice.

Well, there are "dice." But these many-sided gizmos don't look like any dice I've ever seen.

"They're polyhedral dice," I was told by Darvish.

"You're a polyhedral best friend," I told him in reply. I don't know what *polyhedral* means, but if it means small, spiky, and far too concerned with numbers, then my rejoinder is right on the money.

"Rex?" asks Iggy Graminski. "What do you do?"

What do I do?

It's a question that holds more import than his workaday mind can know. I see dead animals. I solve their murders. I am like Sherlock Holmes, Batman, and Ronald McDonald all rolled into one. But I don't think that's what Iggy Graminski is asking.

"What do I do about what?" I ask.

He slaps himself in the forehead with a pamphlet about dragons. "About the bugbears."

Oh, right. I am under siege by bung-bears.

"I am still murky on the convoluted rules," I say, seeking clarity. "What are my options?"

"Anything, Rex," says Holly Creskin. "You can do anything!"

"I can flee for my life?" I inquire. "There's not a rule against that?"

Iggy Graminski nods. "You can flee."

I look to Darvish for guidance. "Can I just hide?" I ask.

He chuckles. "Yes, Rex. You can hide."

Daniel Grimmer lets out an impatient huff. "OR... you can slay every last one of them!"

Dimitri Bellingham grips my shoulder. "You've got this, Rex." Turns out, he is not a rogue after all. But apparently, he is a dwarven ranger named Klaus Roundbow.

Whatever that means.

I look around the table. These people wait with bated breath. Hanging on my decision. Enthralled with the outcome of my action. I am used to this.

I glance across the table to Sami Mulpepper. She flips her rose-tinted locks and grins at me. "Go for it," she tells me. "I've got your back. If things go south, I'll heal you."

And something tells me that she does indeed have my back. I turn to my GM.

"I slay them," I declare with authority.

"Well, you can't just slay them," says Iggy Graminski. "You have to roll the dice to see if you hit."

"To the abyss with the dice!" I proclaim. "I slay every last bung-bear!"

"That's not how it works," says Sami. "You have to roll the dice."

"This game has no dice!" I trumpet to the heavens. "Only these weird, spiky, many-sided numbered things!" I think I'm finally doing it. I think I might be role-playing.

Darvish reaches out and stuffs one of the little objects into my hand. Its many sharp points dig into my palm. "You have to roll the twenty-sided dice to see if you hit," he tells me.

"Roll it!" cries Holly Creskin excitedly.

"Roll it," instructs Iggy Graminski.

"Roll it!" squawks Daniel Grimmer in frustration.

I stand. I hold my fist aloft in a silent prayer to the patron saint of rogues. And I fling the "dice" with force. It pings off the table. It pongs off the wall.

And it lodges one of its twenty spiky points right into Iggy Graminski's enormous forehead.

Sami Mulpepper lets out a snort. I nod with satisfaction.

I'd call that a hit.

Darvish isn't often right, but I have to give him credit. This game isn't half bad.

Suzanne Plunkett

AARON REYNOLDS

is a *New York Times* bestselling author and has written many highly acclaimed books for kids, including *Fart Quest, Dude!, Creepy Pair of Underwear!,* and the Caldecott Honor-winning *Creepy Carrots!* Aaron lives in Chicago with his wife, two kids, three cats, and anywhere between zero and ten goldfish, depending on the day.